Toy City

Toy City

LEE DONG-HA

Translated by Chi-Young Kim

Koryo Press, a division of Yeong & Yeong Book Company
St. Paul, Minnesota

Koryo Press, a division of Yeong & Yeong Book Company
St. Paul, Minnesota, U S A
www.koryopress.com

13-digit ISBN: 978-1-59743-201-6
10-digit ISBN: 1-59743-201-6

Cover design by Ann Delgehausen, Trio Bookworks
Interior design by Stephanie Billecke

Library of Congress Cataloging-in-Publication Data
Yi, Tong-ha, 1942-
  [Changnankam tosi. English]
  Toy city / Lee Dong-ha ; translated by Chi-Young Kim. -- 1st ed.
    p. cm.
  ISBN-13: 978-1-59743-201-6 (pbk.)
  ISBN-10: 1-59743-201-6 (pbk.)
  I. Kim, Chi-Young. II. Title.
  PL992.9.T616C513 2007
  895.7'34--dc22
                                    2006100510

Manufactured in Canada
14 13 12 11 10 09 08 07   1 2 3 4 5 6 7 8

Toy City originally published in Korean under the title *Jangnangam Dosi*,
© Lee Dong-ha, Korea, 1982.

The translation and publication of Toy City *have been made possible by
the generous support of the Daesan Foundation.*

Translator's Note

Toy City, a poignant coming-of-age story of a fourth-grade boy named Yun, depicts the life of a poor family struggling to survive in the years immediately after the Korean War. An autobiographical work, this three-part novel is written entirely from young Yun's point of view. While the political ramifications of the Korean War are suggested throughout, they do not take center stage in this tale of a boy forced to grow up quickly to support his family. Yun copes with tremendous losses, but manages to find joy in everyday occurrences. Lyrical, passionate depictions of hunger, shame, and frustration are interspersed throughout the descriptions of children's games, Yun's budding sexuality, and the kind acts of neighbors, illuminating the conditions under which poor Koreans lived after the War. Vacillating between bitterly ignoring his family and remaining close to them, Yun struggles to come to terms with the sudden realization that he cannot depend on his mother, father, and older sister for anything. Stunningly capturing the wishes, hopes, and anger of a young boy, *Toy City* is a graceful study of the vulnerable toughness of a child thrust into a chaotic early adulthood. Alternately heart-wrenching and hopeful, this masterpiece is a must for those interested in the impact of war on everyday life and the underclass of 1950s Korean society.

Politics and the Korean War are merely alluded to in *Toy City*—rightly so, as the narrator is a fourth-grade boy. Lee Dong-ha's conscious effort in relegating such important issues to the background is unique among his peers. Korean writers of his generation, having experienced the trauma of the Korean War and the division of the nation firsthand, usually focus on these life-shaping events. As such, many Korean novels are driven by political motives to understand, recreate, and contextualize the consequences of the war and the division of the peninsula. *Toy City*, while solidly placing the narrative in the political environment of the mid 1950s, just after the Korean War, and touching on sexual politics and class issues, refuses to make politics a central issue. It is clear, however, that politics fuel the story and the characters. The family must move to a new city, presumably due to Yun's uncle's political beliefs, and Yun cannot bear to look at war amputees because he smells a rusty gun in their presence, an allusion to pacifism. Yet, the main focus of *Toy City* is one boy's dreams and desires. As the novel progresses, Yun's innocence erodes quickly but not completely, as his interactions with adults and other children awaken him to new revelations about life. It slowly becomes clear that a deep, bitter sorrow is quietly hidden under Yun's brave demeanor.

By pushing politics aside, *Toy City* is all the more poignant, powerful, and approachable. English readers will appreciate its subtlety and grace, especially Lee's strength in depicting a child the way children really are, filled with unquenchable energy and inexplicable fear. As coming-of-age stories prove to be more and more popular in the American market, this easy-to-read but sophisticated novel is sure to find many fans, not only in the Korean Studies departments at universities, but also in the general public.

part 1

Toy City

School Performance

My family left our hometown when I was in the fourth grade. I believe the war had ended a year or two earlier. I remember this period pretty well because of our school performance, which was finally held that year. It was usually an annual event but had been skipped for several years because of the war. At that time, the school performance, along with sports day, was one of the biggest events of the year, especially for a school in the country. Because of significant parental interest in the performance, it seemed to be a festival for the entire village rather than a school event.

We practiced the performance diligently for a month before the curtain rose. The fourth grade had planned three programs: a chorus, a children's story, and a children's play. There might have been one more—a dance, in which only several girls must have been involved. I participated in the first three of these productions.

The children's play "Donkey for Sale," into which we poured our hearts and souls, was in our Korean textbook. If my memory serves me right, it was Chapter 8. During rehearsals, we would burst out laughing at the foolishness of the father and son on their way to sell the donkey. That effectively ruined the rehearsal. The kids, nervous until then, would unleash their laughter at the same time. The kids playing the foolish father and son would lose control, and even the kids disguised as the donkey would roll around in their brown blanket, laughing and laughing. Teacher was the only person who never cracked a smile. A gangly man nicknamed Long-headed Locust, he would stand quietly looking out the window until the hurricane of laughter subsided. At these moments he looked as tall as a tree. One by one, the kids would stop laughing and look beyond Long-headed Locust's shoulder. We would rediscover the bright summer sky and fields, and fidget.

When the laughter died down completely, a strange stillness enveloped our hearts. The kids, who had been laughing with impudence, suddenly couldn't say a single word, as if they had all become mute. Some lost themselves in the lush summer scene outside the window, and some thought about secrets from the day before, but we would all passionately wish that this ridiculous and awkward business would hurry to an end.

"The audience should be laughing, not you kids," Teacher said every time, turning around as slowly as a long-headed locust in your palm would, looking more gangly than usual. "You can't do anything in the world if you laugh and cry whenever you want. It's especially true if you want to entertain others. That means you yourself can never laugh or cry. It's wrong and people find it distasteful. Now, let's start from the beginning. Anyone who laughs this time is going to clean the toilets until the school performance is over."

With that, we hurriedly collected our minds, which we had sent out the window. The kids playing the donkey pulled the blanket over their heads and the foolish father and son took the donkey's reins. I stuck the long pipe in my mouth, fingered my beard, and, along with the two other boys disguised as old men, waited for the father, son, and donkey to come toward us. It was an awkward and strange mimicry of life.

Chorus practice was easier than the children's play. Long-headed Locust was a good organ player, though it was too small and old for his long, stick-like limbs. The music that came out of that organ was more mysterious than anything else in this world. Twenty-odd kids were divided into three parts to harmonize for "Cuckoo's Waltz." Teacher, stuck to the front of the small organ and playing with long fingers befitting a man with long arms, looked exactly like a long-headed locust, but nobody laughed at the sight. We didn't have the leisure to laugh—we sang with such gusto that we could barely breathe by the end of the song. Sometimes a very weird voice cracked out and ruined the harmony. At those moments, giggles would burst out here and there, briefly mixing in with the chorus. But Long-headed Locust never took his fingers off the keys. Instead, he pecked at them even more forcefully.

The school would be empty by this time. The summer sunset would seep behind the large ginkgo trees lining the small spring and the Chinese arborvitae fence as tall as we were. Only the few upperclassmen remaining at school listened to our singing. In the calm of the early evening, in which nothing moved or made noise save for a few birds that flew across the sky toward the sunset, only our cheerful singing filled the heavens and the earth.

Most kids went home after chorus practice. Only the day's cleaning monitors stayed behind, making a fuss as they straightened the desks and chairs. But I was always the exception. I had to practice reciting the children's story.

It was lonely and boring. In the deserted teachers' office, sitting in one of the vacant chairs, I started on the memorization. Dark blue seawater danced before my eyes when I opened my Korean textbook and flipped through its well-thumbed pages. The story, titled "Gold Fish," was about an old, kind fisherman, his greedy wife, and a strange gold fish.

"A long time ago, an old man and woman lived by the sea. The old man went out as usual and threw a net into water clear as a mirror. Then he carefully pulled in the net . . ." I had read this hundreds of times already. The long story, with every sentence and preposition in place, was imprinted in my head. I was sick of it because Long-headed Locust made me reread it three or four times at every practice. And he didn't allow me to read it in a quiet voice.

"What are you doing? Who asked you to chant a Buddhist invocation? The people at the back will think they need to come forward with a donation." Long-headed Locust would scold whenever my voice became even a little softer. It was a time before microphones were available. The walls of four adjacent classrooms were going to be taken down to create the school performance site. Our voices had to be loud in order to be heard by the audience sitting in the back. Loudly, I read and reread that damn "A long time ago, an old man," to the point that I could have recited it if my mouth fell open while I was asleep.

"Good. Now try it again, this time adding gestures," Long-headed Locust would order, at this point standing in his undershirt with a towel slung around his neck. He was on his way to the spring to wash away the day's fatigue. Slowly leaving the teachers' office, his long limbs swaying, he wouldn't forget to add: "Imagine that there are hundreds in the audience looking at you right now!"

There were only ten or so empty chairs in front of me, but who was I to point that out? I would look resentfully at the back of the sole audience member walking out toward the ginkgo-lined spring and start practicing again. Feebly opening my arms, I would recite: "A long time ago, an old man and woman lived by the sea. The old man went out as usual and threw a net into water clear as a mirror" and mime throwing a net.

Looking at the man-sized long-headed locust, energetically drawing water with a bucket at the spring on the other side of the darkening schoolyard, I would start snickering.

"Old man, old woman, please put me back in the water. I will never forget this kindness . . ."

Freckles and Warts

*I*n the teachers' office, Long-headed Locust handed me a manila envelope. I took it in the confusion of the moment, even though I didn't understand what was going on. A few other teachers were present. A couple of them, brushing the chalk from their hands, kept glancing at me. I blushed without knowing why. Long-headed Locust stuck out his hand suddenly, saying, "When you go there, study hard. Keep in touch . . ."

Now that I think of it, that was the last time I saw the sensitive and memorable Long-headed Locust. Exiting the teachers' office with the manila envelope in my hand, my nose suddenly stung. The long and narrow hall was chaotic with kids. It was the end of the school day, and they had spilled out of their classrooms in hordes. A few were in my class. They were so familiar to me, having studied together in the same classroom, facing the same blackboard. Where else in the world would there be faces as dear to me as theirs? I knew all of these kids so well, from freckles studded on a nose to ringworm scars hidden under bristly hair, to warts on the back of a hand.

The hall was slippery. The wooden floor, rubbed with pieces of candle and polished with dry rags, was as clean as Mother's hair on the morning of Buddha's birthday, smoothed with camellia oil and coiled into a bun. Slowly, I started sliding along the floor. This was a forbidden game, as you had to be very quiet indoors. Tiptoeing by, some kids gave me disapproving looks, but I didn't care. I slid all the way down to the end of the hall, turned, and slid back. But not a single kid interfered with my reproachable behavior. The hall soon emptied and I was the sole lonely boy left, a manila envelope under my arm.

I was discouraged. Downcast, I stopped sliding. There wasn't a single person in sight. Something crumbled in my small heart. I realized it then—I had wanted someone to interfere. A fourth-grader like me or an older student would have been fine. Then I would have told him: *Look, I'm not going to see you again. You know why? I'm transferring to a school in the city* . . . And what else could I have said? Perhaps I might not have been able to say even that. It was hard for me to deal with—not to mention understand—the fact that I was transferring to a school in the city, and thereby torn away from my school, friends, and familiar world.

I left, tiptoeing obediently. I walked as slowly as possible but the hall ended too soon. Rather than feeling regret, I felt that everything was pointless. Outside, the sun shone brightly. Several kids were playing energetically in the schoolyard, but I didn't go near them. I left through the school gates without dawdling.

The next day our family left the village. Father had been the village head for the past few years and Mother had more relatives here than anyone else. But not very many came out to the outskirts of the village to wave goodbye. Mother kept dabbing her tears away on the sly with the end of her stiff broadcloth skirt. Huddled next to me and our belongings on the moving truck, she seemed small. I couldn't reveal my excitement because of her sadness.

I understood Mother's feelings a little. One night, a group of men suddenly came to our house. Surprisingly, the leader of the group was a policeman we knew. He worked at the township precinct and was friendly with Father. But he had brought violent, bloodthirsty strangers with him. They were so rough with Father that it pains me to think about it even now. That night, they left empty-handed after ripping apart our house. In the end, they couldn't find Uncle. Mother was probably thinking about the events of that night as she dabbed her eyes.

In contrast, Father was calm. He laughed gently as was his habit, even as he said goodbye to the village elders. It was an unrestrained laughter, the kind that, if Father were laughing in any home in the village, people could identify whose laughter it was as they walked by.

Father climbed up next to the driver, who immediately started the truck. Our departure was swift. The village's thatched roofs and the dense leaves of persimmon trees got farther and farther away from the truck, and then they were hidden behind the mountain curve. Swaying with the movement of the truck, I started humming some song, probably a popular wartime tune. I thought back to the school performance: receiving passionate applause for the children's play, chorus, and children's story created by taking down adjoining walls of the classrooms, filled to the brim with villagers. How poised I was! I remembered with pride the words someone had shouted at the end of my recitation: "He's going to be the mayor of the town. Mayor of the town!" Our great mayor himself, sitting dignified in the VIP seat just below the stage, had nodded and smiled as if in approval.

Large sycamore trees stood in rows on each side of the national highway. The truck rattled through that green tunnel carrying the future mayor of the town, whose voice soon grew hoarse.

Toy City

*L*et me describe my first impression of the city later. The first
thing I looked for upon our arrival was water.

The journey was shorter than I had expected. We entered the
city a few hours after leaving our village. I was a bit disappointed
because of that alone. Until then, I had been imagining that the
city wasn't as near as it really was. The city had to be far, far away. It
would have to take one day and one night to get there, even on an express train as fast as the wind. But our mode of transportation was a
rattling moving truck. And even that only took a few hours . . . That
the city was so close seemed like some sort of flaw. *The kids would
be sitting in the classroom now. The fourth-grade classroom where warm,
fresh sunshine came through the south windows, along which spindle trees
were lined up like soldiers, and from which you could hear the continuous
stream of Long-headed Locust's low and gentle voice. Only my seat would
be empty. The sixth desk in the second row from the window . . . Someone
might be looking at the marks and scribbles I left on it, envying me a little
for having moved to the city.* But anyone could easily come to the city
if he wanted to, because the city was a lot closer than I had thought.
My ego was bruised somewhat.

Instead of water, Father handed me money. It was a red one-won bill, small and colored like a maple leaf. I instantly ran out into the main road. I saw a punch vendor with a glass jar bigger than a fishbowl on his wooden cart. The punch jar was filled with ice chunks and all kinds of fruit pieces. I exchanged the bill scrunched in my hand for a glass of punch, colored a deep orange. The cold touching my palm heightened my thirst, but I didn't drink it. Actually, my chest was burning more than my throat because of the wonder and excitement of the city and of city life. I turned slowly, gingerly holding the glass. I took a couple of steps. My foolish behavior being unacceptable, I was quickly stopped.

"Hey, where are you taking that?" asked the punch vendor. I blushed. *I'm doing something wrong.* I couldn't answer. "You have to leave the glass. You just got here from the country, right?"

I emptied the glass in one gulp. I couldn't breathe. My nose tickled and my chest felt tight. But I couldn't dawdle any longer. I returned the cup hastily as if I were throwing it away and ran back to my family, out of breath.

Our belongings were piled high in the alley. The old-fashioned chest that had sat at the edge of the main room in our house in the village, the old wicker trunk that had stood on the guest room shelf, the gourd scoop and wooden rice chest, various clay pots and bowls— these things, placed haphazardly in the alley crammed with shacks, struck me as alien. All of our belongings looked different and seemed to be colored differently from the way they had been in the country. A few strangers—our new neighbors—were helping my busy parents.

I huddled down against a plank wall. I tried to recall the taste of the punch, but I had forgotten. My heart was heavy and I felt dizzy and nauseated. Objects in front of my eyes swayed strangely. *We moved*, I mumbled to myself, feeling ambivalent. *We moved to the city.* I yawned weakly and looked around. Shacks lined the streets densely. Pieces of cans and other cheap materials covered the low roofs. Eaves jutted out into the alleys, touching one another. The many alleys were dark, narrow, and muddy. Hunks of half-burnt coal and black coal dust littered the ground. The residents went about, their accents and outfits diverse. Neighborhood kids had deeply tanned faces, hands, and feet. My dizziness didn't disappear, and in the end I threw up the contents of my stomach. It was exactly one glass' worth of orange vomit.

After bringing in most of our belongings, my family ate an early supper. Actually it was also a late lunch. In either case, it was our first meal in the city. The rice was yellowish, as if dyed with orange-colored water. According to Father, it was because the water wasn't clean. That water, brought in from the public pump, had a sickeningly bad stench.

"What did we expect? The pump is installed less than a yard away from the sewer," Mother kept muttering. She didn't look eager to pick up her spoon. "Eating this is like drinking sewage."

But I was starving. And, despite everything, it was precious white rice. I took the first bite and chewed carefully as if I had never eaten rice before. On the tip of my tongue, I sensed the smell of iron—no, the smell of rusted iron. I put another spoonful in my mouth. My stomach started roiling, the way it did when I had drunk punch.

By all counts, it had been a tiring day. We went to bed so early that we didn't even need to turn on the lamp. Our new house consisted of a single room. Surrounded by planks, from the floor to the walls to the ceiling, the room seemed more like a big wooden box. There wasn't enough room for the four of us to lie down with our legs stretched out. I chose to put my mat and blanket on the low chest at the edge of the room and sleep there.

Tired, everyone fell sound asleep. But I couldn't sleep for a long time. I felt uneasy, trying to sleep floating in empty space. My insides weren't resting easy either. On top of it all, I could hear the neighbors on the other side of the plank walls all night long. The old chest creaked every time I moved. At one point I briefly dropped off the heavy, deep cliff of sleep, but strangely, at that instant, I had a thought—*maybe we've accidentally moved to a toy city*—and smiled.

The Smallest Possible
Space for Everyone

I went to the toilet on the outer edge of the neighborhood three times that night because of an upset stomach. It was a public toilet used by all of the shantytown residents. For some reason, this plank building was painted entirely with tar. So it gave off a terrifying feeling, like a midnight visit to a cemetery. Father came with me the first time. He probably had no other option since I didn't even know where the toilet was. Anyway, I was able to finish my business calmly. *It's probably the water,* Father said to himself as he waited for me to come out of that filthy building. Words cannot describe how reassuring it was to see the red tip of his cigarette glowing in the dark.

But I had to go alone after that. Just thinking about it made my chest constrict. I tried hard not to go. Mother gave me a matchbook and a candle stub. I kept dawdling, gripping my lower stomach with both hands. I couldn't hold it in any longer. The urgency of it pushed away my fear. I left our room looking like I was marching to my death. The moon was bright that night. The half moon hanging in the sky cast a pale blue light over the roofs of the toy-like shantytown.

It was a vivid landscape, like a stage onto which no one had yet come out. From time to time, the sound of people snoring drifted out from the low eaves.

I walked down the narrow, many-forked road as if fumbling in a maze. My hands were slick with cold sweat by the time I finally found the building. By then, my urgent need to go to the bathroom had vanished. I crouched there for a long time, holding the lit candle, but I couldn't go. My stomach was fine, only my legs were cramping. The flame danced, and with it swayed my giant shadow. Once in a while, the old wooden building creaked. It was such a creepy sound that strange associations kept coming to me. For example, the Egg Ghost. The one that supposedly doesn't have eyes or ears or a nose, whose face is smooth save a mouth . . . I remembered the incident well. Dreary winter rain was falling that day. It happened in the bathroom of my school. When a girl suddenly screamed, a few boys in my class claimed that they had seen the Egg Ghost. My legs trembled even more now as I recalled that day's terror.

As soon as I returned home, huffing and puffing, and lay back down, I had to go. I wanted to die. *Damn it.* I blamed the water and this damn city. But finger-pointing didn't solve anything. I would have gone right then and there if I could have gotten away with it without being whipped by Mother. I left again, dawdling.

It was my third trip, all within an hour or two. Maybe that was why, but my terror subsided a bit. Thinking that this smelly building would be my first friend in this city, I did my business calmly. Even though I'd brought a candle nub, I didn't light it this time. Through the crack in the door created by a fallen strip of wood, I was able to see the outside bathed in bright moonlight.

At that moment, someone walked in. I couldn't have been more surprised if a real Egg Ghost had popped up. I almost screamed. It was a woman. Her slip and her long hair, hanging in disarray, had frightened me. I feared she was crazy, and that pressed heavily on my already scared heart. But I soon realized my error. Her appearance was nothing strange, considering she had come out here in the middle of the night. I wondered whether she also had recently moved to the city. *So that's why she's got an upset stomach like me. She'll probably have to come back at least three times.*

Of all booths, she chose the one almost directly across from mine. She lit a match to the candle piece she had brought. *She's doing the same thing I did.* I smiled bashfully. She put the candle down gently in the corner and slowly crouched down. It was an unexpected situation. I looked down quickly, my face suddenly hot. A feeling different from terror overcame me. I hadn't meant to look. She had just been careless. But I was overwhelmed with fear, as if I had done something wrong. I couldn't breathe. I remained ducked down, almost as if I were dead.

After a while, I felt a bit calmer. But I was still scared. I feared what would happen if she noticed my presence. *She might slap me.* Would she believe me if I told her I hadn't meant to look? She might demand to know why I didn't make any noise and lay low so quietly. Then I would say that I hadn't seen anything, that my eyes were closed tightly the whole time. What would she say then? She might still be mad and tell me it was entirely my fault. She might start yelling at me. *Little bastard, delinquent, dirty little snot, bad seed . . .* Now a completely different sentiment started to slowly assert itself. *Why is it my fault?* I was the one who had been so alarmed because of her rash and impudent behavior. *So none of this is my fault.* I looked toward her cautiously, my curiosity, armed with an appropriate excuse, raising its head.

Her door was still open. She picked up the candle stub that she had placed in the corner. I was again enveloped by fear. I didn't breathe until she moved out of my field of vision. Unexpectedly, her face, revealed under the dancing candlelight, was that of a teenage girl.

The next morning, I belatedly felt ashamed of the night's experience. Returning from the public toilet, Mother said, blushing, "What kind of neighborhood is this? I know it's a public toilet, but there's no separation for men and women, and it's not enough for all of these people. Standing in line for that long for that kind of business isn't something a human is supposed to do . . ."

We did learn after a while that there were a few more toilets in our neighborhood. But it didn't matter which one you went to during the morning rush. We always saw people, young and old, wearing uncomfortable expressions, as they stood in long lines holding bits of toilet paper, waiting their turns.

"In this place, it's not only difficult to eat, but it's also a big problem to shit. We're no different. We just have to lay it out in the open, like everyone else," Father said, laughing good-naturedly. Mother blushed again, and only then was I humiliated about the night before.

Butcher-block Desk

I went to school with Father, after waiting for my upset stomach to settle. This was three or four days after our arrival in the city.

Western Elementary School was in the western outskirts of the city. It took us over half an hour to get there, even though we walked briskly. The school and the yard were perched on a shrub-patched hill. The single-story wooden building reminded me of our shantytown. Apparently it was a temporary school. American soldiers had taken over the original school, situated near downtown.

Like our shantytown, the classrooms' floors and walls and ceilings were all made of wood. Similarly, the roof was covered with pieces of cheap aluminum. The rooms were like large rectangular boxes. Some had only walls, with collapsed army tents covering the dirt floors.

We completed the transfer procedure by handing over the manila envelope given to me by Long-headed Locust. Father parted with me in front of the teachers' office that looked like the headquarters of a field army, and I went into my classroom with my teacher.

"You're in class fourteen of the fourth grade," he said, and I was petrified. In my old school, there were only six classes in the entire school, with one grade to each room. I had thought that all elementary schools were like ours.

But a bigger surprise was awaiting me inside the classroom. From right in front of the lectern to the back wall, the kids were crammed in tightly, like canned sardines. I learned later that they numbered more than one hundred. Because of the dearth of classrooms and the uncontrolled increase of students, two classes had to be conducted in one room. There were two teachers. Roll call and the final session with each teacher were done separately, but the lessons were together. One teacher raised his voice in front of the blackboard while the other walked around the room with a switch.

There were many other things that surprised me, like the butcher-block desks. Just like their name, they resembled long butcher blocks. There were no chairs. The kids sat on the floor, four to one desk. Though long, there wasn't enough room to put a single pencil case on it if four textbooks and notebooks were out and open. *So this is what the refugee school is like in the city*, I thought with renewed wonder.

School ended after the fourth period. The kids pushed out of the room. It was chaotic. The teachers yelled and brandished the switch without mercy, but couldn't keep them under control. Like caged wild animals discovering a hole through which to escape and rushing out en masse, the kids cavorted untamed.

I stayed back until the end. Of course, I was intimidated, but my legs were also cramped because they had been folded for such a long time. I left the room slowly, after most of the kids had gone. I crossed the yard, from which tree roots protruded, and walked into the noon sunshine. The school gate was a gate only in name. A sign with the school's name was hanging from one of two stone mounds.

A group of rascals caught me right after I passed through the gate. They had doubtlessly been looking for a chance to pounce on me. There were four of them, and they were too big for me to believe that they were all in my grade. I was easily dragged into the shrubs where I was beaten up. I didn't put up any resistance. They stopped only when my nose started to bleed. One of them said, "You're not even a kid from this area, are you? And you're not a refugee either, right? That's why we beat you up. You're just a lame hick. You better remember that!" He patted my back in a friendly manner, and I couldn't do anything but nod. I sniveled, wiping away the sweetish blood trickling into my mouth.

From that day, I started to divide people into three groups. Though I learned this by paying the valuable price of self-respect, it was an experience that allowed me to understand the world a little better. It was true. In our city, three types of people lived together: the natives of the city, the war refugees, and people like my family, who had left our hometowns for shameful reasons.

Seoul Kid, Onion Bit

Tae-gil was my first friend in the city. He was a refugee, originally from Seoul.

Kids made fun of him with this chant:

Seoul kid, onion bit
Tasty whale meat
Why did you come
Crossing the Han River bridge?
He came here wanting to eat
Whale meat, onion bit

Sometimes like a slogan, sometimes like a song, the kids repeated these words. Then Tae-gil would get mad and run around, trying to catch one of them. But he usually couldn't catch anyone. The neighborhood streets were a maze. There were many places to run to and hide in, and it wasn't a big deal even if Tae-gil caught someone. Actually, there were some who would purposefully get caught once in a while. It happened if they played the game in an alley with few passers-by, or if it grew tiresome. Then Tae-gil, contrary to his earlier behavior of running passionately after them, would quickly become disappointed and stop. He would just breathe hard, curling his hands in tight fists and glaring at the other kid.

He was clever. He calculated that he wouldn't have a chance of winning by fighting with the tough kids. It wasn't only about numbers. He was weak, perhaps congenitally. He was tall but all bones. I was nervous whenever he ran after the kids. I worried that he might snap in half at the waist, like a dry millet stalk. At those moments I thought about Long-headed Locust, since Tae-gil looked like a baby long-headed locust.

Tae-gil and his eccentric mother lived nearby. I don't know whether it had always been just the two of them or if they had lost other family members on their way to this city. I remember that Tae-gil himself never said anything about this matter.

There were good reasons why we thought his mother was strange. First, it was her appearance. Though in her forties, she always looked fresh and neat. She looked like she was going out even though she spent most of her time inside their box-like room. Her careful bun shone with castor oil, and two eyebrows, resembling thin moons, were well-drawn above her splendidly made-up features. Her rubber shoes and traditional socks were as white as snow. She was different from the other women, who wore roomy pants and covered their heads with a towel. I remember Father saying that she must have worked in a *gisaeng* house before. "That kid Tae-gil is probably the product of some bum."

Guests came often to Tae-gil's house. They were rumpled men in their fifties. Sometimes they came in a small group, other times they came alone. If he weren't sent for liquor or cigarettes, Tae-gil killed time in the alley. If you asked him who the guests were, he would just reply that they were from Seoul. He never clarified whether he and his mother knew them from when they lived in Seoul, or whether they got to know the men after moving here. Anyway, the guests drank or played cards for hours and then left quietly, which also struck us as something that made Tae-gil's mother eccentric.

But the way she treated Tae-gil was the definitive reason for our opinion. There was hardly a kid in the neighborhood who didn't get whipped. They were beaten by their parents or perhaps by their older siblings, and that was the only way to protect them from all sorts of danger. Hardly a day passed without the echo of sobs of a caned child ringing in the alleys.

Even so, the beatings were severe in Tae-gil's case. Not a punishment-free day went by. For him, a beating was like daily bread. If the neighbors started wondering, *maybe he won't get a beating today*, then, as if in answer, his wild cries would suddenly burst out. He would often get his share in the middle of the night, when everyone was in deep sleep. His neighbors, jolted out of sleep, would grumble a bit or smile bitterly and yawn, turn out the lights, and go back to bed, finally assured that their sleep would no longer be interrupted that night.

Tae-gil was as petulant as he was clever. Everyone smiled, listening to the varied sounds he emitted while being beaten. Screaming, sobbing, begging for forgiveness, all of which he performed with perfect drama, made it seem like the mother and son were involved in an amusing game. When he ran out of the house naked from the waist down, even the most stoic person couldn't hold back his laughter.

But his mother was even more clever. Tae-gil's dramatics never fooled her. She was as cold as she was clever, and never accepted her son's exaggerations. She put down the switch only after applying it, as methodically as if tallying numbers, to his skinny long-headed-locust-like body for the amount equaling his wrongdoings. He often ran away in the middle of a whipping, but he always returned on his own two feet. He had to endure it anyway, and couldn't look forward to any peace until he received his daily share. So my friend Tae-gil would face his mother's switch again with an unbelievably sad resignation.

Of course, the fault was entirely his. Tae-gil had nicknames other than Seoul Kid Onion Bit. Bunting, Diving Beetle, Wooden Cart, Mister Know-It-All, Waterfowl's Bottom, etc. All of these names implied his frivolity and cleverness. He got involved in mischief big and small, and these things were worthy of beatings in his mother's eyes. It was unfortunate and tragic. But then everyone's life was filled with misfortune and tragedy. Of course, his mother wasn't considered to be eccentric just because of this. We thought she was odd because of the particulars of her beatings. Why did she make her son take off his pants before whipping him? If it were only for the whipping, it would have been sufficient for him to just roll up his pants. And it was a foolish way to do it if it was to safely keep the guilty party there until the end of the appropriate punishment, because the young offender would often run away with his dick dangling. After a lot of thought, our conclusion was that his mother was an eccentric. Because she was weird, she beat him like that, and because she beat him like that, she seemed even stranger.

Tae-gil had a single abundant freedom: he didn't have to go to school. His odd mother oppressed all of her son's freedom, but she couldn't have been more generous when it came to this issue. I couldn't understand it for the life of me. I envied him. For me, there was nothing more difficult than going to school, as I had gone through such an ordeal on my first day. My head pounded just thinking about the ramshackle building on the hill, the sardine-can classroom, and the rough, shrewd, and rowdy kids.

Tae-gil was lucky. I would have given everything up to have a little bit of his freedom, even if I too had lost my father and had only an eccentric mother. Once, envious, I asked him why he didn't have to go to school. Tae-gil replied confidently, "Why would I go to that stupid refugee school? We're going back to Seoul soon."

But nobody else stayed in that alley as long as they did. Later, when my family left, he was still there, eagerly helping us move.

Bun Tin with
Twenty-four Holes

Father had said that in this city, it was not only difficult to eat, but also to shit. Father still maintained his calm when he said this. But how could the difficulty of doing one's business, despite having to line up in front of the public toilet every morning, compare to that of eating? Father couldn't solve this problem even though a month had passed since we had moved here. Nothing is more difficult than feeding one's family. During his almost forty-year existence, a few *majigi* of land was the only thing that Father had depended on. At least dirt was a straightforward opponent, never betraying Father's honest hands. But the opponent facing Father now couldn't ever be trusted. As honest as Father was, he was incompetent.

One day, around the time I realized that we must have gone through what money we had, Father brought in two appliances. One was a bun tin, and the other was a punch jar. I'd often seen the latter in the streets, but I had never encountered the bun tin before. The cast-iron tin had twenty-four holes, carved in orderly rows.

Even a bowl of cold water wasn't free in city life—you had to pay for every little thing. My family learned the cold-hearted order of city life during that one month of inactivity. It was pointless to wonder what Father had been thinking coming to the decision to sell food on the streets. This was obviously his first and last investment.

While we looked at the appliances with curiosity like they were magic lamps, Father announced heroically, "Now, we're going out to the streets tomorrow. And we're going to make some money with this bun tin!" Nobody wanted to criticize Father's simple optimism. We too had big expectations. Nobody dared to say it, but we hoped with fluttering hearts that the tin would be more than a mere bun tin—that it would be a machine that would print twenty-four bills at a time.

The next day my family went out. Taking over a corner of a busy street, we hung the tin on an apple crate. We made a fire, prepared the batter, and took out the red-bean paste. Of course, all of this was done by trial and error. Father's hands, used to handling dirt, were clumsy. Every time he made a mistake, we giggled, which helped ease our embarrassment and awkwardness.

It was midday by the time we produced the first buns. As Father took one of them out with trembling fingertips, we heard the noon siren go off, stirring the air heavily. We each took a bun following Father's example, studying every inch of it. It was cute and bright yellow, like a newborn chick. We had probably added too much gardenia dye, Mother analyzed. Sister pointed out that the red-bean paste had leaked out and judged that the batter was too watery.

"Next time we'll be more careful. Now, why don't we taste it?" Father said, and we all took a bite. Nobody said anything. Everyone exchanged looks, diligently savoring the taste.

"How is it?" Father asked cautiously. None volunteered an opinion. It was as if our mouths were glued shut. Hot, sweet, and with a . . . bitter aftertaste. How would one evaluate this? It was the first time in our lives we'd tasted this sort of food.

"The aftertaste is a bit bitter . . ." Father said finally. He looked stumped.

"Yes, it's a little odd," Mother said, and we children agreed, cautiously.

"I think there's too much saccharin . . ."

"Don't you think we used too much baking soda? It tastes just like that."

Disagreeing on the cause, Father and Mother went back and forth a few more times. But the conclusion was that the buns were bitter, so the conversation soon died.

It was embarrassing to sell the buns when the reviews were so mediocre. But it was the first time we were doing this. The fire burned away and the tin, greased with perilla oil, was ready. And we even had an earthenware tub filled with batter.

"It's not bad and it's definitely edible. Let's just make buns out of this batter today," Father finally decided. We got to work. Sister made the buns and I lined them up to make an enticing display and sold them. The operations went smoother than expected. Sister kept producing twenty-four buns at one time, and I had a lot to do since it was lunchtime. I also tasted the buns here and there, so I was pretty busy.

Father set up shop across the road. It was easy to become a street vendor. Already all sorts of fruit pieces were in his glass jar. Mother poured in a bucket of water, and Father bought a big chunk of ice and put it in. All they had to do was to wait for customers.

I looked across the street when I had fewer customers. I couldn't see Mother. Under the shadow of a handful of small weeping willows stood the wooden cart, the large punch jar on top of which several glasses perched, and Father, his straw hat pressed down on his head. He poured punch from a yellow rubber hose and searched every pocket to find enough change for a customer. Sometimes he smoked peacefully, looking out indifferently at the city's empty sky, and at other times he would be lost in thought, often dozing off. Father, who had only ever dealt with dirt, coped with the dishonest and untrustworthy city in this manner. Even now, that picture is etched deep in my memory, like a watercolor.

Feast

My family had a feast that night. Since it was opening day for our business and it had been one month since we'd moved here, the feast was a meaningful event. First, Mother brought in a low table. Sister wiped it clean with a cloth and neatly lined chopsticks and glasses on it for each of us. A dish of *kimchi* was placed in the middle. We were ready. Mother stepped across the threshold into the room, wiping her wet hands on her skirt, looking like she was wondering what she had forgotten to do.

Mother examined us as she had always done. Looking carefully at her children sitting at the table, she checked to see if we had dusted off our clothing and if we had washed our hands and feet well. Because it was so late, and our excitement of the day's events hadn't yet settled, our appearances were unsatisfactory overall. But Mother didn't say anything. That had never happened before.

Finally, Father came in carrying a big bamboo basket filled with the buns we had baked earlier, arranged in an appetizing way. Mother put it on the table. Sister, taking the kettle, carefully filled our glasses with the punch left over from the day's sales. A few fruit seeds floated around.

The atmosphere was peculiar—a little hollow, a little awkward. But the mood wasn't annoyed or sad. We just didn't try to look at one another. Looking downward, we picked up our chopsticks silently.

"O.K., let's eat. It's late, so we'll just have to eat this for dinner tonight," Father said, as if announcing the start of the feast, and put a whole bun in his mouth. He picked up his glass. "They say Westerners eat bread every day, so why can't we eat it for a meal or two? If we were still in the countryside, we wouldn't be having such fun . . ."

I selected a bun and popped it in my mouth, just as Father had done. It was cold and hard. But I chewed diligently, washing it down with lukewarm punch. I realized that the things we kept producing all day were mere buns, not bills that Father had been hoping for. *We might fail at printing bills in the future.*

By the time my family lay down side by side, like matches in a box, we could hear our tired neighbors' snores through the plank walls.

Tough Widow, Her Daughter, and Her Son-in-law

I woke up suddenly. It was the middle of the night.

I just lay there for a while, my mind blank. I thought I had heard something. Even though it was for a mere instant, I had heard something very abrasive, which brought to mind the sound of something scratching against steel. Perhaps I had heard it in my dream. Right then, the high, sharp sound—a shrill female voice—came again. "What the hell are you two doing in the middle of the night? Just be quiet and go to sleep!"

My consciousness, which had been lost between sleep and waking, finally found its bearings. The voice had burst out from one of the three neighbors sharing our walls. I wasn't the only one who'd woken up. My entire family did, and so did our neighbors, whom we could hear rustling. Father found a cigarette and lit it, grumbling. The match briefly illuminated the darkness.

Sleep was long gone at this point. I listened quietly, lying face down on the low chest, looking down at Father's cigarette glow. Someone was crying very privately. It was the kind of weeping that came from suppressing wild emotions with all one's might. It gave the listener an eerie feeling.

"Why are you fighting under the covers? Are you enemies now? If you're going to do this, just break up, break up now!"

The situation was obvious. The shrill, screaming woman was Tough Widow, famous for her dirty mouth, and the one weeping quietly was her daughter. The only obscure part was that there seemed to be someone else other than the mother and daughter. But the third person didn't say a single word. Tough Widow's curses and her daughter's crying were the only sounds that streamed through the walls.

With manly square shoulders and abnormally large hands and feet, Tough Widow had only a daughter when she came to the neighborhood. This hadn't changed, but now she always had a man around. Her daughter was more feminine. She was fragile, often sick, cried a lot, and had a pale face. She apparently worked at a bar of some sort. Coming home late at night, chased by the curfew, she was frequently so drunk that she wouldn't be able to walk straight. Often, near midnight, I would look out through the hole in the window at her walking down the empty alley, completely intoxicated. A few worthless types would creep behind her, sometimes whistling boorishly, and each time she would raise her alarmingly thin arm and flick them off.

But she couldn't do that every time. Plus, she was now about twenty years old, a sensitive young woman. One day, despite her mother's insistent interference, she'd brought one of the worthless guys home. He was good-looking—light complexioned and neat. It wasn't only she who had pinned her hopes on him. Even I, unrelated to them, harbored great expectations of him. I thought that Cinderella had finally found a wonderful prince.

But he was a powerless prince. A lazy loafer, he lay around at home, and she was an unlucky Cinderella, returning late through the shantytown alleys drunk, harassed by other worthless bums. Soon the sounds of their fights started coming through the walls. They were fights between her and the fellow, between her and her mother, or between Tough Widow and her son-in-law.

Tough Widow's sharp curses and her daughter's weeping didn't stop. The loafer still didn't make a peep. Then again, what could he have said? A useless bum, he would have nothing to say even if his mouth were as big as a jar. I wondered what he looked like at that moment. I imagined he would look like a guilty puppy driven under the porch.

"Mom, I want to die. I really just want to die . . ." the daughter cried, and her mother's fury became more and more pronounced.

"I don't care if you die or not. Why are you complaining to me, when you're the one screwing around? This is my house. Leave, both of you. I don't want to even look at you. Why should I live with you and have to worry? I don't care if you die in a pit or if you fuck day and night. So just leave, you monsters!"

I can't record all of Tough Widow's heavy, persistent abuse. In any case, their relentless commotion disrupted the shantytown's exhausted slumber. Suddenly, we heard the guy retort, "Why won't you give me your pussy? What kind of man would be happy to just live with a bitch who doesn't give it to him?"

This was the problem. Laughter burst out from here and there. Mr. Gwak, the secondhand dealer, known to be a wiseacre, said loudly so that everyone could hear, "The man is right, of course. A man who lives with a bitch who refuses sex is worse than trash," and guffawed.

Toy Room

Plenty of neighbors other than Tough Widow's family robbed the residents of their exhausted sleep. The drunkard Ju, who lived across the alley from us, would wake the neighbors because he was a bad drunk. Like everyone else, he was a man filled with bitter regrets. It was believed that he had crossed the 38th Parallel a few times to bring with him the family he had left up north. But he was alone by the time he arrived here, after his many life-endangering adventures.

Ju was a skilled carpenter, so his earnings were decent compared to others'. But this was yet another misfortune in his case. While his neighbors were obsessed with finding daily nourishment, he, along with his good earnings, was holed up at a stand-up bar. He left reluctantly only after the hostess turned his pockets inside out with greedy, rake-like hands, looking for the last bit of change.

The alleys looked narrow even to a normal person. What would they have looked like to a reeling drunk? He returned home swaying, hitting his forehead on the walls on either side of the alley, with a saw, a carpenter's square, and a hammer sticking out sideways from the top of the loose mesh tool bag slung over his shoulder. I was always enveloped by a strange curiosity when I bumped into him in that state. It seemed like a single stream of cool liquor would burst forth from his drunken body, but that never happened. Even when he smacked his face head-on on the plank walls, he would become wet with blood, never liquor. Instead of being disappointed, I would be touched. Now that I think about it, wild emotions more intense than liquor swirled in his body. An excruciatingly painful remorse for the past and a bottomless despair for the future . . .

Ju's strange drunken habits emerged when he finally arrived home. He would lock himself in. Then, the sound of his belongings being smashed to bits would leak out from behind the closed door. His bad habits had started.

He had a wife and a son of about five or six years old. They had met after he'd come to this neighborhood. According to the neighbors, he appeared at this shantytown a few years ago and became the head of his current family a couple of years later. Obviously, he was the boy's stepfather.

Nobody could deter him from his habits. Amazingly, his wife and stepson never said anything. Only the sound of things being broken could be heard. Sometimes the noise persisted throughout the night, and then his undeserving neighbors wouldn't be able to sleep. Even Mr. Gwak didn't crack jokes about Ju. Instead, he would call someone else loudly. "Hey, Mr. Kim! Let's talk about life. How's business at the Yankee market these days?"

The reply would come through the plank walls, and sometimes a third person would chime in from another side, and a late night conversation would take place for a while.

"Whether the economy is good or bad, I think I might get rich quickly."

"That's good. Although it might be a bit uncomfortable for some-one like that to live in a neighborhood filled with beggars."

"You're talking about the good old days. Let me in on the action, too. Just wait and see. The world left me like this but I'm a good man. I'm from a pretty good family."

"What are you doing, Mr. Yi? It's a bit suspicious that you aren't saying anything."

When we looked into Ju's house the next morning after a sleep-less night, we would find it in ruins. Except for the outer wall and the floor, almost nothing would be left in its place. The strange fam-ily would be eating breakfast amicably amid the devastation. As soon as they were done, Ju would make noise again, but this time an ener-getic musical variation of reconstruction.

As I said before, he was a skilled carpenter. His talents were well used in reconstructing what he had destroyed himself. From the alley, people could hear Ju asking his wife's opinion, cutting, shav-ing, hammering, and resuming his habitual humming. Only then did the neighbors feel safe to look into Ju's house without hesitation. The construction progressed in an orderly and thorough fashion. The room took over the kitchen area and the kitchen was built where the room had once stood. The overhead storage space on the east side was hung on the west, and the small porch on the west side was moved to the east. With genuine amazement and envy, everyone watched the creation of completely new and different living quarters from those of the day before, in the same limited space. For Ju, who had lost everything, his wooden box-like room might have been the only world and the only toy granted to him.

Blanket

S ummer nights were unbearably hot. Everything got on our nerves—our stuffy box-like room, the burning coals taken out to the narrow alleys for cooking, the stagnant, rotting smell of sewage, the swarm of mosquitoes that went wild as soon as the sun went down. During summer nights, living itself was annoying.

Sister and I often went out to the street to sleep. At least it was ventilated there. We felt so expansive lying on top of our wood cart, a dyed army blanket pulled up to our chins. The dark sky was boundlessly wide and soft. The stars were so twinkling and bright that our hearts would become damp with starlight.

At times we would be woken up and chased back home. But usually people looked the other way. If I opened my eyes in the middle of the night, the stars in the sky would be in different places. If I woke up again, after having fallen asleep without realizing it, the stars would be tilted to one side of the sky. Moment by moment, the summer night sky looked new.

Many others came out to the street to sleep. If I awoke in the middle of the night and looked down the street, the neighbors, lying all around, looked white under the moonlight. After midnight, the street resembled a garden strewn with fallen pear blossoms. A baby would whine next to its sleeping mother and someone would be sitting up alone, smoking and lost in thought. Nothing could disturb our sleep. The curfew thoroughly regulated all such possibilities. Cars of the privileged raced past, flinging dust onto our sleeping faces, but we didn't care. The street was calm at night, amid the people's exhausted slumber, in an oppressing and fragile peace. I could almost hear the night dew falling like soft rain.

One night, feeling a chill, I opened my eyes. It was dawn. Morning approached silently from the far side of the street, herding damp grayness. I sat up. I was bare. I woke Sister, who also had nothing covering her. My throat closed up suddenly.

"Hey, where did our blanket go?" Her voice oozing with moisture, Sister looked around.

I replied in a low voice, almost whispering, "It's gone, Sister. Someone must have stolen it while we were sleeping . . ." My voice, trembling from the dawn chill, came out weakly.

"What are we going to do? What are we going to do?" Sitting in her shabby underclothes, Sister started crying. But with some kind of dampness clogging her throat, she couldn't make even a small child's whine. I stared blankly at the sky. Sister's dry and narrow forehead was becoming visible in the early morning light.

Rainy Season 1

The rainy season started in the middle of the steaming heat. The narrow alleys quickly became a quagmire. Squirming worms crawled into our room.

When I woke up in the morning, my world was completely wet. The walls, the ceiling, the straw mat-covered floor of the room, and our belongings; all of these were soaking wet. The flimsy roof, covered with cheap materials, leaked wherever a nail was hammered into it. The sound of rain dripping into empty cans, washbowls, and chamber pots made me feel melancholy, like listening to a rusty xylophone.

We lay around most of the day, since there was no reason to be busy. We didn't earn very much even on a clear day. The buns still tasted bitter—we couldn't figure out why—so our sales were below our expectations. The only thing we could trust was our own mouths. Dinner frequently consisted of buns. But we never again experienced the awkwardness and empty feelings we had felt during our feast. We only felt the nauseatingly bitter and sweetish aftertaste of the flour, yeast, baking soda, and saccharin mixture. Usually Father's earnings weren't that great either. Sometimes he could barely afford to buy ice chunks. Every evening, Father poured the remaining punch into the sewer in front of the house. Then the stale sewage turned a pretty orange, and the sweetness diluted in it floated around the alley all evening. Father didn't mind eating the buns but hated that scent. After the feast, we never again had punch at our dinner table.

The rain kept falling. We couldn't have sold anything even if we'd dragged the wooden cart out to the streets. So my family spent almost the entire day shut up in that box of a room. Lying down with a damp blanket pulled over my head like a cocoon, I couldn't have been more aware of the rain pounding on the flimsy roof and the thin walls. The rain, drenching the entire universe, finally soaked into our souls. Lightly dizzy and lucid from hunger, we enjoyed the sound of water pooling on the ground.

This was the rare time when Father hummed. He never sang out loud. Perhaps it was to ease his heavy heart. I could hear only a few measures through his low, thick, nasal humming. Father would repeat the simple, flat tune for a long time, pausing in between, as if chatting with someone invisible.

The song that Father sang over and over again was such a familiar one. Father was humming the rice-planting song in that toy-like city.

Rainy Season II

Nothing was more annoying than trudging to school in the rain. The way to school was long and muddy. There, those monstrous kids were sitting cross-legged at each butcher-block desk. The knowledge two teachers could impart to all those kids didn't amount to much. Maybe that was why the teachers always doled out more whippings than knowledge.

But I never cut school even when I sold buns with Sister. I was first and foremost a student. Sure, I enjoyed helping out, but it didn't occur to me to drop out of school, which wouldn't have been acceptable anyway. My parents still had certain hopes for me. Their hopes for my future were probably their only comfort since leaving our hometown. Their pet theory was that living in the city was more beneficial in educating children. *It's hard to educate kids as a poor farmer.* I had to remain a student, if only for them. Helping Sister was possible only in my free time. However, I did have a premonition that I would have to quit school one of these days because of our situation.

I had to go to school through what seemed like a series of swamps. I was able to get to the hill on which the school stood only after passing an empty lot with muddy water collected in it, a treeless park, and following a slippery, serpentine road along a rice paddy. A trip that had taken 30 to 40 minutes took over an hour in the rain. Very few students held black, sturdy umbrellas. Most only had field jackets made of dyed army raincoats, which they pulled over their heads. I didn't even have one of those, so I draped a piece of nylon cloth on my shoulders. When I walked through the rain in that outfit, it felt as if our entire city was built on a gigantic bog. And I was a resident of this city. I yearned for a straw raincoat from the country but was glad we had not brought one with us, as it would have looked strange in these streets.

The school didn't have running water. A single pump stood in one corner of the yard. The kids stood in a line in front of the pump in the order of their arrival. You could go into your classroom only after you cleaned your shoes and feet, which always looked like you had just crawled out of a muddy rice paddy. The line was long and joyless, the way a refugee train is. And since it was difficult to work the pump, the line inched along slowly.

Two big kids stood on each side of the classroom door. They were monsters, little gangsters. They were gatekeepers who had been given an enormous power by the teachers. They judged us confidently and harshly. Being barred from the classroom because you were still dirty was horrifying even to imagine. Many kids weren't allowed in and had to go back to the end of the refugee train in the rain. Some had to go through that ordeal three or four times a morning.

I didn't want to do anything to make them cross with me. Having clean shoes and feet didn't guarantee that I would enter the classroom. Numerous possibilities for an accident existed between the pump and the classroom, and it wouldn't have mattered even if I were that man from Nazareth who walked on water. The gatekeepers exercised absolute authority on such decisions. I too experienced the indignity once: despite going back and forth between the pump and the classroom to make my feet as clean as shrimp fresh out of the water, the monstrous little gangsters had declared my disqualification.

I wasn't strong but I also wasn't foolish. I didn't want to be the object of ridicule ever again. The secret to passing the inspection was clear and simple. All you needed to do was to give the hungry pack of wolves something to eat. In my case, I had access to unlimited resources. My family always had an abundance of leftover buns, of which we never sold as many as Father wished. I could bring to school five or six of those buns, left over even though my family ate them every day, sometimes at every meal, almost until we got sick of them. The rascals became tolerant of me. Once, since my clearance seemed automatic, I sailed past them confidently without first stopping at the pump and was punished harshly by the teacher.

By the time we sat down in front of our butcher-block desks, there wasn't a dry thing in sight. You couldn't have gotten that wet even if you had just crawled out of a pond. Our clothes, books, and notebooks looked like they had been dipped in water. Moisture pooled around our bottoms on the wooden floor, so the teachers went around barefoot. They wove between the kids without slippers or socks, the legs of their pants rolled up. At least it was summer. It would have been perfect if we could have pushed all the desks to one side and received swimming lessons. But we were never granted that kind of fun. To me, the teachers seemed like the leaders of those little monsters.

Soldiers' Cinema

Someone passed me a note, which I opened under my desk. 'Meet us in front of the soldiers' cinema!'

One of the monsters had sent it. I ripped the note into tiny shreds, and it melted away quickly on my wet palm.

The soldiers' cinema was on the top floor of the town hall. I didn't know why it was called the soldiers' cinema, since you could go to it even if you weren't a soldier. Students and civilians made up the majority of the audience. You could enter for the price of several glasses of punch, and they always showed two features. The films were pretty old, but sometimes they were as well kept as those of a new-release theater. But the presence of a film interpreter excited the audience the most. He looked like a soldier. His short hair, the words printed on his undershirt, and the color of his pants all suggested it.

The facilities were rundown. Every corner was saturated with the smell of sweat, urine, and dampness, and the long wooden benches were uncomfortable. The cinema wasn't well ventilated. During the intermissions, the stale air would feel heavy, like a sticky liquid being whipped. Two large fans made a frightful noise. But when the lights went out and the film started, the cinema became a palace loaded with children's dreams, adventures, violence, and tears. We clapped tirelessly for Anthony Quinn, the pirate leader, and cried for Elizabeth Taylor, the princess of tragic loves. We were fascinated by the war hero Audie Murphy, by Burt Lancaster, Gary Cooper, John Wayne, Richard Widmark—the dignitaries of Western gunmen. Anyone would have quickly realized how impressed and moved we were by watching us as we left. The expression in our eyes suggested we had lost everything in an instant and our feet were unmoored, staggering; nothing else remained with us.

The rascals were waiting for me. I thought I would have to buy tickets for all of them. But I couldn't. Not only had I never had that much money, but I also wouldn't be able to get my hands on that kind of cash any time soon—the rain still poured down, soaking the streets. I didn't expect the rainy season to end for a while. I prepared myself to meet their demands with my body, like my first day at school. But I had miscalculated. They already had the tickets, including mine. One of them said, "We had a few promotional tickets. That's why we told you to come."

I didn't understand what he meant. I just assumed that the entrance tickets were also called promotional tickets. Anyway, we entered and watched the movie. It was great fun. Anxiety raised its head from time to time, but I would soon lose myself in the movie again. I started to feel nervous when the two features were over and the lights came back on. I had given everything to the darkness. I only had a suddenly empty heart, where the shadow of anxiety was deeply cast. I thought that they would demand something from me, and that I would have to pay more than I'd expected. I felt deflated, like an empty sack. I probably looked as if I wanted to be filled again with enormous emotion and wonder. The kids picked up on that.

A painter's studio was on the roof of the town hall. A few independent signboards were propped up in front, getting wet. The kids talked in low voices there for a bit, and then came outside. It was still raining. Little by little, damp darkness spilled out from the far side of the road. One of the kids began to whistle expertly, but the rest didn't say much. In truth, we were starting to feel hungry, so we peered into Chinese bun and *udon* places. It might have been because of the rain, but the kids looked sad and depressed.

Before parting ways, one kid handed me two tickets. Then he spat out abruptly, as if he were annoyed, "Let me know if you need more."

I took them wordlessly. Big letters spelled out *promotional ticket*. I couldn't figure out how he'd managed to get hold of them, or why he was showing such goodwill toward me. I stood there dumbly, holding the lucky—or perhaps unlucky—tickets. Their gloomy eyes watched me. Finally, I offered, "I'll bring a lot of buns tomorrow, enough to fill up a shoe pouch." That was, of course, a lie. I hadn't offered them a single bun for the past few days. There was no way my family could go sell anything with the rain still coming down. Things wouldn't suddenly change tomorrow. Lately, instead of eating leftover buns, my family had started having dough flake soup for dinner, something I couldn't offer to the kids.

But I spoke again. Some emotion, not just nervousness, made me lie through my teeth. "I can probably bring some Chinese buns. We're planning to sell those, too . . ."

We could see the sign of a Chinese bun house across from us. It was an authentic Chinese bun place, their buns made by a Chinaman.

Eyeing the shop, I waited impatiently for their reactions. Rain kept falling, moistening the darkness. I felt an unbearable hunger.

One of them opened his mouth, breaking the dejected mood. His voice was shockingly weak. "Forget it. You don't need to bring us that stuff anymore."

Turning around, they dispersed. Alone, I stood dumbly in the wet darkness. A strange loneliness gradually filled my empty heart. It was a loneliness I'd never experienced before. This might have been what the Western gunmen felt.

Fallen Fruit

I went to gather fruit with a group of kids. The seemingly never-ending rain was coming to a halt.

I don't know who first thought of it, but we believed that there would be mounds of unripe fruit, felled by the constant rain, piled in the orchard outside the city.

We each took a sack and headed to the orchard. Clouds were scattered dizzily in the sky and rain sprayed down intermittently. Wherever you looked, you could see that the rainy season was ending. Our hearts were light with happiness. We chattered like birds and frolicked like young wild animals. We joyfully sang a variety of songs, from Sunday school hymns to popular songs of the time. As soon as someone started singing the first verse, it became a chorus. We were so preoccupied that we didn't realize where we were going, or even how far we had come.

It was past noon by the time we got to the river, which had swelled enormously. Red, muddy water had filled the river's width and was streaming by. We stopped in our tracks as a matter of course. It was the first decisive hurdle of the trip.

The suggestions were divided into two opposing factions. One argued that we should continue, while the other insisted that we head back. Both sides had good points. The faction arguing for advancement said: *Even though the river's wide, it's shallow and slow. We could definitely cross it if we wanted to. How could we turn back now? We've been walking for hours. We'll get to our destination if we just cross this river. Look, that green forest you can see across the river is the orchard. And tons of fruit are there.*

But the opposing side was persuasive as well. *Still, it's impossible for kids like us to cross the river. What are we going to do if there's an accident? One measly sack of fruit isn't worth it. It's too bad, but it makes more sense to turn back empty-handed.*

We came to a conclusion after a debate that was as noisy as a flock of sparrows. But it was quite a compromising decision. We decided that those of us who were confident should cross it, and that those who weren't should stay back and wait. On one condition: we would split the goods equally.

One by one, the bigger kids in our group crossed the river first. As expected, it wasn't very deep and the current was weak. But it wasn't an easy adventure. I joined the first faction. The water came up to my belly button. The bottom of the river was composed of drift sand, so it was like crossing a bog. By the time I made it to the other side, I was more worried about the return trip than I was looking forward to collecting fruit. Collapsing weakly on the sandbank, I regretted that I had jumped headfirst into this imprudent adventure.

A few girls in the group crossed the river last. They were a few years older, bigger, and taller than we were. I thought they would have an easier time navigating the river. But they were indeed girls. Their expressions all changed as the water came up higher.

My sister laughed the entire time. When the water rose to her calves, she laughed that the water was at her calves, and when the water went above her knees, she giggled that it was so. But her laughter didn't come from the ease of mind. She was only expressing her nervousness that way. But her friend wasn't like that. She waded through the river quietly, like the shadow of a mountain. She didn't look at my sister, who was laughing continuously. She hoisted up her skirt as the water came up higher, concentrating solely on the progression of her feet. The river became deeper, and her skirt was pulled up higher and higher. I was soon enveloped with a strange tension. I felt a strong urge of some sort but my mouth was glued shut.

By the time the girls got to the middle of the river, my intense expectations had come true. It was already too late when Sister's friend realized her mistake. It was only for a split second, but that didn't lessen her humiliation. She hurriedly pulled her skirt down, lost her balance, and swayed.

Less than half of the group had crossed the river. We started off again. From afar, we could see the sour citron tree fence that surrounded the orchard. The kids let out an excited roar and ran toward it, their empty sacks fluttering behind them like flags. Strangely, the most excited and talkative person was that girl with the skirt mishap.

We returned like victorious soldiers. It was around evening, and the narrow, muddy shantytown alleys were filled with coal smoke. Our war spoils were fallen fruit, as small as tiny sour citrons. They were still sour and unripe, but they were fresh presents to us. It's hard to know whether some of the kids mentioned that skirt incident during their late dinners. But it's certain that the memory wouldn't easily be erased from at least a few of our heads. The girl looked very downcast when we all left. She held a half-full sack, but she wasn't interested in it any longer. She looked like she was lost in thought, her suddenly miserable face pointing downward.

I was the first to turn away from her. Walking home, I suddenly remembered something. It was her. She was that girl I had seen in the public toilet the first night we arrived here.

Where Is He Now?

Summer had almost gone by the time the rainy season was over. Cold wind constantly blew through the cracks between the plank walls. In the sewer, which used to stink in the middle of summer, the beautiful chirping of insects struck harmony with the moonlight. For the toy city residents, who didn't have anything to harvest, fall was a sad season, like water that is cold to the touch.

The bun tin with twenty-four holes had rusted over. The taffy seller took it away. Sister was sad and Father didn't say anything. I was more interested in the dry millet stalk-like taffy sticks for which we had traded the bun tin. Even the taffy seller didn't want the punch jar. It had had two big cracks from the beginning. We could have used it as a fishbowl if we'd repaired it with bandages, but we didn't have room for it. In the end, we threw it out in an empty lot. Father was silent then, too.

We had only the wooden cart left. Mr. Gwak gave us a good price for it. Father bought a secondhand bicycle with the money. He rode out on it in the morning and returned late at night. He would be empty-handed when he returned home, the same as when he left.

We would have steamed millet for breakfast. If you poured water over it, each grain scattered like sand. It was hard to eat without dropping some, no matter how careful you were. Mother was upset every time she wiped the table after the meal. The precious spilled kernels amounted to about half a spoon. She always lectured us with the same words: "At least wild animals would take them in the country. They're just going to rot in the sewer here." I never pointed out that the worms in the sewer would eat them.

Sister ate only half of her portion for breakfast, leaving the rest for lunch. That way, she felt as if she had had enough. I couldn't understand it for the life of me. For me, that was impossible. I tried it once or twice, following her example, but I wasn't satisfied at either meal. It wasn't enough for breakfast and I was still hungry after lunch. I wanted to feel full at one meal at the very least, instead of feeling hungry at both. So I usually waited until dinner to eat again.

The lunch-less days felt longer. I had to make myself busy to fill this vacuum. Tae-gil often took care of filling our time. Running around together all day, we became inseparable. We went to the sawmills and took the bark off logs, collected coal bits from the coal yard at the train station, and added water to powdered coal and shaped it into long, thin briquettes. Later—of course it was only sometimes—we graduated to bringing sawdust instead of bark, whole rock-hard coals instead of bits, and square coal briquettes instead of powdered coal. Anyway, our efforts supplied fuel for our two households.

But one can't eat fuel. I would return home after a long, hard day and our room would be the only dark one among the many makeshift shacks crammed tightly together. I could read the day's situation from Mother's and Sister's eyes. Warm water waited for me in the kitchen. I would scrub my hands and feet quietly for as long as possible, as if I could wash away my hunger along with the dust and fatigue. Then I would lie quietly down beside Sister.

We wouldn't be able to fall asleep, even though it was late, the moonlight shining brightly through the hand-sized window. Because the moonlight was so clear and pretty, our hungry selves would feel transparent, too. We waited for Father with hearts as clean as water. Even sleep couldn't encroach upon us.

I would ask quietly into Sister's ear, "Where is he now?"

Then Sister would turn toward me and reply like a small child, "He's 10 *ri* away."

Sister's breath gently tickled my earlobe. Comforted by that feeling, I would ask again, "Where is he now?"

"He's 5 *ri* away."

"Where is he now?"

"He's at the railway embankment."

"Where is he now?"

"He's in the alley."

"Where is he now?"

"He's at the door."

I would sit up slowly, thinking I heard Father's bicycle. Then Sister and even Mother would look out as well.

There were times when Father's return coincided with our game. I can't express with words the deep emotion we felt at such moments. Once, Sister even started weeping quietly with gratitude. It was fine even if Father came home with nothing in spite of our expectations. I couldn't imagine a more perfect reward than his return.

But those times were extremely rare. In most instances, we saw only the ill-fitting narrow door and the early autumn moonlight drenching the discolored window paper. If we were lucky, we could also see a star or two through the window. Father wouldn't be home yet even if we played the game a couple of times in a row.

Sometimes, we would suddenly be woken up in the middle of the night. By the time I got up, rubbing my eyes, Father would be sitting near me, wearing the same clothes he had worn in the morning. Mother would bring something in from the kitchen. She would whisper to us before we picked up our spoons, "Eat quietly without scraping your bowls. Drink some water first."

We would start eating stealthily, like thieves. If our spoons clinked, we would become petrified. But Father wouldn't be careful about being noisy. He ate almost nothing, but he made the most noise that might disturb the neighbors, and later he would even say, "Everyone who comes to the city becomes a beggar at least once. They say that you find your way only after you eat up everything you own, even every particle of dust . . ."

It wasn't just Father's words. Feeling some strong emotion that made my throat close up, I was starting to realize something. What we waited for so ardently was Father, not something that would fill our hungry stomachs.

One of You

The monstrous kids were called to the teachers' office all at the same time. The teachers followed soon after. Orders left by each of the teachers were scribbled as if in annoyance on the blackboard, threatening the remaining kids.

"Study quietly!"

"You'll be in big trouble if you talk!"

But these weren't kids who would be intimidated by that. More than a hundred mouths started talking. The class quickly turned into a waiting room in a train station.

I put my book and notebook on my butcher-block desk and opened them, but didn't feel like studying. The person who sits quietly in a waiting room is actually the strange one. Right now, the popular thing to do was to talk. The kids chattered about the monstrous kids, and as many details were recounted as there were mouths. The story line was more or less the same. As I had myself realized, they were apparently monsters, small gangsters, and petty thieves. Someone who remembered the indignities of the rainy season said that they were small tyrants and no-good sheriffs.

I was confused. I remembered the time I went to the soldiers' cinema with them. I still hadn't understood their behavior. Why did they invite me, and why did they give me two promotional tickets afterward? Plus, they hadn't accepted my offer of food, instead saying dejectedly, "You don't need to bring us that stuff anymore."

Their behavior hadn't changed even after that day. They were generous toward me without demanding anything in return. Sometimes, they would speak to me: "Hey, do you want to go to a movie?" "Are you hungry?" I was the one who received things from those boys, even if it was a small piece of bread or a pencil stub. Of course, it wasn't often. As for me, I didn't feel burdened as I had when we'd gone to the movies. I had cautiously concluded that they didn't want anything in return. There were times, though, when I felt a little nervous, and I would wonder why they were being so nice to me for nothing.

I was able to figure out what kind of trouble they were in by listening to my classmates' many stories. They had done something to an older girl, someone I didn't know. I did know the perpetrators pretty well, and I knew that they were very capable of doing such a thing. Although they were in my class, they were two or three years older and bigger. It would have been silly to ask about their temperaments. Everyone said this was such a big deal at school because the victim's father was an important person, but nobody could verify this. It was impossible to know whether the kids, as noisy as sparrows, had invented the details of the incident.

Quite a number of kids were talking about something very different. They said the little gangsters had finally been caught stealing random goods and stationery from a few markets downtown. They had been selling them by force at school. I had witnessed several coercive sales myself, so this story also seemed convincing.

I thought either one or both of the two stories could be the cause of today's events. The kids kept chattering like birds, and some ran boldly around on the desks. The room, which had been filled with humidity during the rainy season, was now thick with dust, as if it were a construction site.

The teachers came back after a while, but the gangsters were nowhere to be seen. I assume that they never returned to that classroom. I don't know anything more than that, because soon after I also bade farewell to that memorable refugee school on the bare hill.

One of the teachers ordered us to stand up on our desks with our pants rolled up. The desks creaked and groaned with four people's weight on them. But it put our calves at a perfect height for a whipping.

Pointing at the letters written on the blackboard, the teacher shouted, "Can't you read yet? Don't you know what 'studying' means? Or do you not know what the word after that means? Why are you kids even here? Do you think this is some camp for war orphans?"

The other teacher had already started the whipping. You could hear brutal sounds from the back, but nobody dared to look. We were like live, trembling fish, placed on large butcher blocks.

The first teacher, realizing that words were of no use, started caning the kids as well. He started with the first row. The switch was severe and fair. Red and blue snakes crawled across our calves displayed on top of the desks. The room was filled with the sound of the switch cutting through air, the explosive, dense sound of it meeting flesh, and the kids' screams and sniveling.

The room was filled with a strange heat. It felt hot, heavy, and muddy. It seemed as if a very long and dreadful time had passed before the teachers met up in the middle row. They hesitated briefly, in front of the last kid's calves. It wasn't for very long, but it must have seemed like eternity for him. We all waited nervously, because an exception wasn't possible.

One of the teachers let go of the switch. The other dropped his as well and brushed off his hands. Surprisingly, that kid was the only one pardoned.

Back at the lectern, the teacher couldn't catch his breath for a while. His hair was mussed and sweat glistened on his forehead. He was so tired and washed out that it was hard to believe that he had brandished the whip like an emperor just moments ago.

Looking at us sitting on our knees in front of our desks, the teacher started to speak. His voice was soft and exhausted. But his words struck our injured hearts more than ever. "It's a dark and confusing time. I trust that you will grow up well nevertheless. I want to keep you safe and not lose a single one of you, even if that means I have to whip you every day. So later, when you look back on these days, don't ever say that our whippings saved you. I want you to remember that there is one person here who wasn't whipped." Saying this in one breath, the teacher turned his back to us and slowly erased the board.

I don't think we completely understood the teacher's words. But we felt its truth in our hearts. A few kids sniveled in the solemn silence, and the teacher started writing on the now-clean board. I think it was about an experiment conducted with peas.

On the way home from school, I bumped into the rascals. I think they were waiting for me. They were all depressed. They looked scruffy, like kids chased out into the streets—which they were. One of them told me that they had to bring their parents to school the next day. His voice wasn't confident. I wanted to ask why, but I didn't dare say anything. I became melancholy too, as if I were a part of their group. Nobody said anything. They just stood there dejectedly, like small gangsters, or perhaps like bums.

"Want to go to the movies?" Finally, one boy opened his mouth.

"Do you have any promotional tickets?"

"We already saw it. Why do you want to see something you saw yesterday?"

"Well, what else is there to do? Are we just going to stand around like bums?"

There was nowhere else to go. We spent the rest of the afternoon at the soldiers' cinema. I was the only one who kept his eyes on the screen. The others each took over a long bench and lay down as soon as the movie started.

It was evening when we left the cinema. The sky had changed into a slate blue. Everything was the same as the last time, except it didn't rain. They still looked dejected, like a street where darkness was creeping in slowly.

They stuck out their hands as we parted. I was sure that they wouldn't ever come back to school. Their hands were warm but their backs looked very lonely. A certain emotion filled my heart to the brim. I finally realized that they were monstrous and gangster-like, but that they had been considering me their friend. They were probably the loneliest kids in the world.

Clerk for One Day

M r. Gwak came by as I was starting to think that I would
have to drop out of school. His friend who ran a department store was looking for a good clerk.

Father wasn't home. Mr. Gwak spoke with Mother for a long time.
I grasped the situation immediately; Mr. Gwak had come here with
me in mind. Mother said I was too young, but he argued that I was a
good, smart kid. "What's the point of school in this situation? It's better to raise him as a market rat if you can't finish educating him. You
should forget about school, since we have an opportunity here . . ."

Mother wiped her tears away with the edge of her skirt. I thought
that it was a foregone conclusion.

The next day, I left with Mr. Gwak. I felt free. The shop was at
the edge of the market in the outskirts of the city. The sign said "Universe Department Store" but the interior didn't fit its name. It was too
small to be a department store, but rather big for a general store.

I was received by the proprietors, a married couple. They were in
their mid-thirties and looked well groomed. Looking me over carefully, they wondered whether I was too young, and Mr. Gwak praised
me as he had done to Mother. The couple smiled quietly in answer.

I was hired. They were to provide me with room and board. They also promised to give me a monthly allowance and necessary clothes, telling me that I couldn't expect more than that right now. They said they would reimburse me suitably in the future. When I grew up, they would marry me off and set up a small shop for me. These were promises that would be fulfilled ten years in the future, at the earliest.

"You're a part of this family now, so be good." Mr. Gwak patted my back and left, looking very satisfied. I just stood there dumbly, feeling ambivalent about it all. I felt as if I were floating in empty space.

What am I supposed to do? I wondered in embarrassment. I looked around uncomfortably like a hick in a government office. All sorts of products were displayed. They each had their own use, shape, and charm. I realized how unappetizing and useless our buns had been. I wandered through the store, looking at the displays. Everything I saw captured my heart and heightened my desire to buy. I wanted everything. From a carved wood tiger to a black umbrella, from a small gold button to a brassiere, I wanted it all. I would have been the happiest person in the world if I could have had every displayed object. Maybe I would be able to achieve this amazing feat in ten or twenty years. I decided that, when the time came, I would ask the owners if I could get that instead of being married off and receiving a shop.

I was still embarrassed when I finished touring the store. I hadn't figured out what to do. The proprietors hadn't asked me to do anything yet. But they were watching me. I felt like I was waiting for someone in a place where I didn't belong. Anxious, I felt my palms turning clammy with sweat. I wished that someone would hurry and appear and take me away from this awkward place.

At lunch, I had Chinese black-bean noodles. It was the first time I'd eaten it. It was so good that I thought the owners had ordered it especially for me. My family had been starving for the past few months: I was always hungry. It was only after I single-mindedly emptied the bowl that I remembered Mother and Sister. My nose stung.

The proprietress said, "The shop has to be clean at all times. You should keep wiping the display case and the floor. Then, go stand in front of the door, and greet customers politely and guide them."

But the shop was already clean. I had never before seen such a clean and orderly place. It was so perfect that I almost thought it couldn't be real. Also, there were few customers since it was around lunchtime. There wasn't much opportunity for me to help anyone.

A few customers stepped in after lunch. I couldn't utter a greeting even though I was supposed to help them. Receiving a warning after they left, I blushed. The proprietress was as kind and as relaxed as she seemed at first, but that warning made me realize my situation once and for all. I was no longer my old self. I was a kid who had been sold for a few promises. Helping customers, cleaning constantly, and running random errands were, no matter how unimportant, my only duties from now on.

I firmly made up my mind to do my job and waited for customers. A young woman came in. Without delay, but with immense effort, I said, "Welcome. How may I help you?"

Once out of my mouth, they were easy words. I approached the customer, more confidently than I had thought possible. She stood there, looking not at the products but at my face. I felt as if I had seen her before.

Mustering up courage, and picking up my foot and making an awkward gesture, I asked again, "How may I help you, Ma'am?"

She passed by me without saying a word. She shouted toward the back, "Sister, are you here?"

I looked toward the back, flustered. The proprietress was looking at me, a smile on her kind face. I felt as if I had missed a step and fallen down. This was how I would be living for the next ten or twenty years. My face burned. I listened to their conversation, my head bowed.

"Is he the new kid?"

"Yeah, he started today."

"Where did you get him? He looks like a hick."

"Seems like it. What do you think? Doesn't he seem innocent but smart?"

"Well, who knows? He might have sticky fingers like that other kid . . ."

It was past 10 P.M. when I had dinner, after locking the shop doors. I was served white rice and a piece of fish. I hadn't eaten this kind of food since the ancestral rites in the country last year. But I couldn't finish even half of my meal. I felt light and calm. I had already come to a decision, after having thought hard all afternoon. I revealed my intentions as soon as dinner was over. The proprietors were disappointed. They tried hard to reverse my decision, mentioning my family's financial situation and even Mr. Gwak's feelings, but I was immovable. Of course, being married off and getting my own store were important. And it was especially very sad to give up the chance of acquiring all of those items in the display case—the carved wood tiger, the black umbrella, the small gold buttons, and even the

brassiere. But I didn't change my mind. I believed that I had to go
back to our unsanitary and smelly box-like room.

Mother didn't scold me when I got home late that night. She ca-
ressed my head without a word, and kept looking into my face. Sister
was very happy to see me. She grasped my small hands repeatedly,
as if she had found a lost brother. She asked me over and over again,
"So, how was it? Did you eat dinner? Did you really?" I kept nodding.
I looked around our poor but immensely cozy room and saw a bowl
of liquor-filtered dregs mixed with saccharin in the corner. I could
smell liquor, the smell of sweet persimmons, on Sister's breath.

The Way a Mute Cries

Father didn't come home for a few days. We were very worried but didn't know how to find out where he was.

Mother didn't move. Lying on the warmest part of the floor, she didn't budge, night or day. But she had always been sickly. Illness could have been her oldest friend. Still, she couldn't hide that she had become weaker recently. If I woke up in the middle of the night, I would often hear Mother moaning in pain. She would be engaged in a painful battle with her old friend while the rest of us slept. But Mother wasn't the kind of person who would take to bed just because of that. We thought this was her way of waiting for Father.

Sister and I would frequently go out to the alley to look for Father. Sometimes we even went out to the big road after the curfew siren had swept by. But our expectations were always dashed. We started to think secretly and slowly that Father might never come back, since it would be too frightening and awful to accept such a misfortune right away.

Cold autumn rain had been sprinkling all day. In the morning, Mr. Choe, the head of the neighborhood association, stopped by. A short man, he was known to bustle about, taking care of neighbor-hood affairs. Unexpectedly he'd brought news of Father.

Only a few words were spoken between Mr. Choe and Mother. But just from that, Sister and I could see that the situation was seri-ous. Mother, hurrying out with Mr. Choe, looked shockingly pale.

It was near evening when we found out what had happened to Fa-ther. Mother came back, completely exhausted. She cried for a while. This had never happened before. Mother never showed her emotions; everyday joys and sorrows never ruffled her calm. Now Mother was crying audibly in front of us. Sister joined in on the sorrow without knowing the reason. My nose stung but I held my tears back. Turning my back on them, I stared at the walls pasted with newspaper pages.

Father was in jail. Apparently he had been caught transport-ing something with his bicycle. Mother didn't know if it was stolen, contraband, military supply, or some black market object. Whatever it was, it was illegal to transport it, so he had to serve a prison term. Father, my honest father . . .

We didn't know where the object came from, or why Father was transporting it. But we were certain of one thing—that the object in question was definitely not Father's. That much was doubtlessly true. We all knew he hadn't had even a single red one-won bill in his pocket for the past few months.

Though the situation didn't change, the moment of shock passed. Mother returned to her normal self. She lay down on the warmest part of the floor and closed her eyes peacefully. What was she think-ing? She must have resigned herself to the fact that Father's bad luck couldn't be reversed. Instead of sobs, hiccup-like sniffles came out. It seemed like our bad fortune had ended along with the weeping. I

thought that this might only be a bad dream. I thought I could see
Father coming home on his rickety bicycle. I left the room silently.
All was quiet behind me.

Some kids were playing noisily out in the alley, making fun of
Tae-gil. I stood there dumbly, like a groggy child just woken up from
a nap, and listened to their chorus.

Seoul kid, onion bit
Tasty whale meat
Why did you come
Across the Han River?
He came to eat
Whale meat, onion bit . . .

They repeated the chant several times, but Tae-gil was silent.
Squatting with his back against a plank wall, which was softly illuminated by the fading afternoon light, he poked the muddy ground
with a skewer. He had received a beating from his eccentric mother.
One by one, the kids dispersed.

I slowly walked through the alley to the big road, but I had no
place to go this late. I stopped and looked up and down the street.
The dirt road was covered in thick dust. A row of military trucks
covered in camouflage nets passed me. I remembered the teacher at
the refugee school saying that this was a dark and confusing time. I
calculated how long it had been since my family had moved to this
ridiculous city.

The spot where Father used to sell punch was empty. Only the
lone small weeping willow was there, its faded leaves covered in

a thick layer of dust. A woman with a towel wrapped around her head was sitting where Sister and I had turned out buns. It was obvious that the woman was a newcomer from the country. Fresh sweet potatoes, only as thick as an adult's finger, were displayed on her wooden tray.

Hearing a strange noise, I looked to the side. A bunch of kids were spilling out of a ramshackle building on the big road, which we called "dummy school." They were around my age, but they weren't from our toy-like shantytown. I knew that they lived all over the city. They were deaf and dumb.

I stood there for a long time, watching them. They scattered away, wildly gesturing with their hands and making their typical strange sounds. I turned back after the last kid left. I pictured my hometown, which I had completely forgotten about till then. I remembered my school, the kids, and the last school performance. We'd sung the "Cuckoo's Waltz" and performed the children's play, "Donkey for Sale." I had received an ovation for my recitation of "Gold Fish" and had been recognized as a future mayor. But now I had become a fatherless child. Sobs pushed up to the top of my throat, but I didn't cry. I was a mute who hadn't learned to cry.

part 2

Starving Soul

Dragonflies

That autumn without Father made me feel as if the entire world were hollow. Our box-like room had never looked so big and empty. Mother spent the fall in bed, which actually reassured me. At least she filled the empty space a little.

Since the beginning of autumn, the neighborhood kids had been intent on trapping dragonflies. They were so focused on that task that they even forgot to make fun of Tae-gil. It was lucky for him, but it had to be an ordeal for the dragonflies.

Most days, the riverside next to the neighborhood served as our hunting grounds. The river, in which clear water must have flowed at one point, was severely polluted. It seemed as if the city's sewage, including that of all the shantytown's households, streamed into this river. I peered into the dirty and smelly water, thinking that the city was rotting from its roots. It was certainly a wonder that such small, delicate, and colorful living organisms would swarm around in that kind of place.

When nothing special was going on—which was always—I spent almost every day by the river. Tae-gil, talented at catching dragonflies, was a good friend for this task. We captured so many dragonflies whenever I went around with him that I would run out of fingers with which to hold them. If you've ever looked closely at a swarm of dragonflies drifting gently through space, with the autumn sunlight trickling amid them like clear water, you would begin to understand how they caused delicate tremors in our hearts. That was part of the reason for my love of catching dragonflies. I held the ones we'd already captured while Tae-gil ran around with the butterfly net. With a dragonfly pressed between each finger, I would stare vacantly at the swarms flying low over the river.

Autumn was the time of year when everything seemed hollow. The blue sky, without a speck of dust, looked hollow, as did the sunlight, as clear as water. At the very least, the war hadn't left a single scar on them. Nothing was hidden. Every object in sight revealed its innards, as if transparent. Was there another organism as transparent as a dragonfly? I was often moved, looking up at the dragonflies shimmering like autumnal sunlight. They had nothing, so their very existence was cleaner and neater. They reminded me of my mother's sickly face.

I studied our captives, their wings pressed between my fingers. The red dragonfly was the prettiest. I thought the reddish paint might stain my fingers. The dark brown dragonfly made me feel uncomfortable because of its triangular black prints. My mood soured whenever I looked at the three spots lined up at the tip of its brown body. I felt the same with the red dragonfly with three black lines engraved on either side of its chest. The brownish female made me feel especially depressed and unlucky. Although it was difficult to find a wheat dragonfly in those days, similarly negative feelings would flood my heart if I ever caught one. I didn't like the white powder covering its body.

I shuddered whenever I discovered its white powder rubbed off on my fingertips. Compared to these, the dragonfly with gorgeous dark brown spotted wings was the most beautiful. I admired the dark pattern clearly etched at the edge of its transparent wings.

But the biggest reason for my fascination with dragonflies lay elsewhere. Despite their transparent wings, fragile and delicate bodies, six long and thin legs, and silk thread-like veins, almost all of them had coarse heads, tough mouths perfect for eating flesh, a pair of big, unwholesome double eyes, and chisel-like chins. Their mysterious paradox delighted me.

Tae-gil returned, looking tired. His net held another dragonfly. To determine who would get the first pick, we played rock-paper-scissors with our feet. He won. I stuck my hands out for his scrutiny. The day's capture was studded, one by one, between my fingers. He chose my left hand. The dragonflies in my right hand were mine. We walked home slowly with the dragonflies nestled between our fingers like jeweled rings. I was so hungry that it was hard to keep my head up.

Mother was still in bed. This comforted me for some reason. Seated next to her, Sister turned to look at me, her face pale. Even in the darkening light, she looked very thin. I leaned against the wall, not saying anything for a long time. *We're waiting for Father to come back on his rattling secondhand bicycle. We might hear his bicycle again tonight.*

"You caught a lot," Sister said. I nodded and slowly released the dragonflies, one by one. They flew dizzily around the small space, in our toy-like room, weakly and transparently as if they were thin hungry spirits. We would never have as transparent souls as they do, even if we only ate grass, even if we only took in the dewdrops dangling on grass stalks.

But I believed that Mother had a transparent soul incomparable to even the dragonflies' wings, since she didn't take in anything but water.

Bread and Words

On Sundays we kids went to church. Almost all the shantytown kids were enrolled in the children's Sunday school. Nobody ever missed Sunday school, not even those who hated the refugee school, nor kids like Tae-gil, who never went near it. On Sundays, we were all diligent students.

The church sat on a hill near our neighborhood. It was a poor pioneering church, consisting only of two large military tents and a small belfry. Thick layers of black coal dust from the blast furnace of a neighboring foundry coated the road to the church and its small yard. The bottoms of our feet quickly became dirty no matter how careful we were.

One of the two tents was reserved for the children's Sunday school. It was sparsely decorated, but then nothing could have survived the hurricane inside. A noisy gang of brats, we took over the place completely. We saw no reason to hesitate. If only for this moment, we forgot our daily bread: our parents' frequent scolding and their frightening switches. At least here, we thought that we had unlimited special privileges that granted freedom from reprimands, and were certain that any act would be forgiven. This was why Tae-gil drew a naughty picture on the wooden floor with the end of a nail and why a couple of kids cut down a length of rope from the tent and used it as a jump rope. Nobody was ever caned or expelled from Sunday school because of that kind of mischief.

Our teachers were always able to command this rowdy herd of sheep with blackened feet, hands, and hearts. It wasn't too difficult to calm us. Smiling, a teacher would say, "Now, let's all sing a hymn. Everybody knows Hymn 110, *Savior, Like A Shepherd Lead Us*, right? Sing loudly if you know it, or softly if you don't. One, two, three!" and vigorously wave his arm. Then we would quickly lose ourselves in song.

"And continue with Hymn 100, *This Is My Father's World*, one, two, three!"

Singing pushed out all kinds of bad impulses from our hearts. We became small, gentle sheep after singing three or four hymns in a row. We also listened to stories of Jesus of Nazareth who was hung on a cross and of his many miracles. We winced collectively when his head was crowned with spikes, and long nails were pounded into his palms. I believe that every last person there felt his pain. Some even screamed, while others dry-hiccupped repeatedly.

Once, an amazing incident happened before our eyes. A girl my age suddenly had a seizure. I knew who she was, since she lived in a neighboring alley. She looked perpetually scared and her face was pale, as if there weren't a single drop of blood in it. She always seemed hysterical. From what I heard, she hadn't been five years old yet when the war started. Her father had been a devout Christian in their hometown in Hoeryeong, in North Korea's Hwanghae Province, and now pushed a cart in a transport company warehouse. It was said that only a big broadcloth sack was slung over his shoulder when he crossed the DMZ, from which he took out the girl. That was how she became our neighbor.

We crowded around and looked down at the small miracle. She lay on her side, her eyes rolled back. Sticky saliva coated her mouth and marble-like sweat beaded her pale forehead. Standing on our blackened feet, we didn't say a word. But we realized that she was sick. She was in so much pain, her small, weak body writhing, that our small hearts felt as if they would splinter like pieces of dry firewood.

Of course, we were told plenty of exciting stories as well, including Jesus' various miracles. We were shocked when he cured a leper, got a paralyzed person to stand, got a mute to speak, saved a child possessed by evil spirits, walked on water, and made a fig tree wither. We admired him. But of all the miracles, our favorite was what happened in the empty field on the other side of the Sea of Galilee. We all cheered when the teacher told us that five loaves of bread and two fish fed five thousand young men, and that the leftovers filled twelve baskets. Some kids stomped their feet and clapped.

"That's not all," our teacher said, smiling, "It also says in the Book of Matthew 15:32 to 15:38: Then Jesus called his disciples unto him, and said, I have compassion on the multitude, because they continue with me now three days, and have nothing to eat: and I will not send them away fasting, lest they faint in the way. And his disciples say unto him, Whence should we have so much bread in the wilderness, as to fill so great a multitude? And Jesus saith unto them, How many loaves have ye? And they said, Seven, and a few little fishes. And he commanded the multitude to sit down on the ground. And then he took the seven loaves and the fishes, and gave thanks, and brake them, and gave to his disciples, and the disciples to the multitude. And they did all eat, and were filled: and they took up of the broken meat that was left seven baskets full. And they that did eat were four thousand men, beside women and children . . . "

We hollered again, and some whistled. Right after that story, we realized we were hungry. The majority of us suffered from chronic empty stomachs. Mesmerized by the feast of rich words, we had forgotten the most important issue for us. We rushed outside, even though the service wasn't over.

A long line formed in the narrow, coal dust-filled yard. Everyone looked tired and hungry. Our eyes, which had been filled with wonder and awe, now glistened with calculation. We waited our turns impatiently, fishing a flour sack or a cement bag from our pockets. Our hunger pangs reached a peak. The quicker kids ran down the hill, having already taken their share. The kids still in line became more and more impatient, so the line kept falling into disorder, even though we all knew that even the last kid was never sent away empty-handed. It was hard for me to wait my turn.

When I finally received my share, I felt a greater emptiness than happiness. I turned around, exhausted, and saw Tae-gil's mouth dusted with powdered milk, as white as a clown's. I could see our neighborhood behind him. I believed that some incredible miracle would take place in that shantytown, slapped together with pieces of thin wood and cans and aluminum scraps. Nothing less than a miracle could rescue my family and neighbors.

I was very tired and hungry, but slowly started to run toward our room where Mother and Sister were waiting for me. Scuffling behind me, Tae-gil scooped out another handful of powdered milk and poured it into his white, clown-like mouth.

Even God Can't Cope

*I*don't know who started doing this, but some of us went to the Catholic church as diligently as to the Protestant church. The Catholics handed out yellow cornmeal instead of powdered milk, and two scoops at that. I coveted it. The three members of my family could subsist on it for at least two days.

Cornmeal was more practical as well. Our stomachs couldn't digest the powdered milk. It didn't matter whether we ate it raw or cooked it. Our stomachs would start to flood over, even with our hunger barely sated. It was hard to move my legs after visiting the toilet a few times. So the powdered milk only serviced our mouths. The cornmeal, on the other hand, was more substantial. Various methods for cooking cornmeal existed, so if you cooked it with a lot of water it became porridge, and if you used less water and let it rest, it became pudding. Sometimes we made yellow, fluffy corn cake, and other times we ground it finely, mixed it with water, and drank it. It was perfect for our daily bread, even if its taste was nothing to write home about.

The Catholic church was far away, in the middle of the city. I hesitated to make the trip because I would have to cross several busy streets to get there. I was still a hick, frightened of city streets. Also,

I vividly remembered the way I was hunted down on my first day of school. I couldn't shake off my anxiety, even though I was going with a group of kids. I thought that traps would be hidden all over the city. I felt like I was venturing into a Mesozoic prairie in which dinosaurs roamed, not a post-war city.

But the biggest reason I hesitated was in my heart. I didn't think it was right to have transactions with both the Protestant and Catholic churches. It wasn't because of different rituals or even doctrines. I couldn't discern fine points between the two, and honestly, I wasn't interested in finding out. I only cared about a small amount of powdered milk or two scoops of cornmeal. Of course, neither the Protestant nor the Catholic church forced you to believe their religion in return for food. Still, there needed to be at least a modicum of discretion. I would have felt the same way even if we'd gone to two different Protestant churches, since I thought that one should be criticized for attending two churches.

For this reason, I was very embarrassed the first day I went to the Catholic church. I thought every pair of eyes could see through my shameful behavior. The long line crept forward slowly. Not only were there kids standing in line, but also young women, mothers with babies, and old grandmothers. This embarrassed me further. Waiting for my turn with my head bowed, I decided I would stop going to the Protestant church, even belatedly. I was sad that I would have to give up the powdered milk, but I was sure that I wouldn't feel ashamed about receiving the cornmeal.

Tae-gil was standing in front of me and looking around, with a bored expression on his face. He suddenly pointed. "Hey, look, that girl came all the way here too."

I looked where he was pointing. The girl who had had the sudden seizure in Sunday school was standing there. She still had a pale, bloodless complexion and looked tired and ill.

"Her father's a deacon at the Protestant church," Tae-gil whispered. I didn't reply. She seemed to weigh as little as a piece of mulberry window paper. She looked like she would quickly become rumpled up among the throngs of people.

Tae-gil was very content with the cornmeal. It was his first time, too. My happiness was no less. The weight of the two scoops of cornmeal slung over my shoulder made me happy beyond description. The cornmeal was promised for the next week as well. I believed that I would receive the cornmeal the week after that too. I ran after the kids excitedly, suddenly feeling rich. I wasn't as self-conscious as I had been before, even when we crossed a busy street. Passersby looked curiously at us, but I decided there was nothing to be embarrassed about. I should bring Sister next week. The girl who had had a seizure followed us quietly like a shadow. For her sake, I unconfidently concluded that her father's god and our new god were probably similar.

But my approval of the Catholic church had been too quick. Actually, I had gotten there too late. Even though it was only two scoops of cornmeal a week, too many needy people had come. By my third trip, the situation had changed. Several pots as big as oil drums took up the churchyard, mass-producing watery yellow corn porridge. It must have been their last resort.

From that day on, we only received the amount of porridge two scoops of cornmeal would produce. Instead of sacks or cement bags, people brought kettles, pots, and buckets. I will never forget the strange glances and smiles people gave us when our group crossed a busy street, porridge in hand. *It's a good thing that I never brought Sister.* Walking home with a big gaggle of kids, I kept thinking such useless thoughts.

"Even God can't cope," one big kid giggled, "I'm sure His pockets will run out soon."

Everyone burst out laughing. I recalled the miracles recorded in the Book of Matthew. No such event ever happened, though.

The Park

The park was ten minutes away on foot from our house. It was the sole park in our city. In it were an archery range, two old pavilions, and a part of an ancient mud rampart, ruined but still standing. It also had a small pond and a stone etched with a poem of a local poet.

But the area was too desolate to be called a park. The trees were tiny and the pond gave off a stench. The severely deteriorated grass, despite its strong ability to regenerate, didn't look like it could return to life. The naked, wretched hills revealed landslide marks. During the war, this park had housed more refugees than the number of city residents. The scars of past ordeals remained on every stone step, on every tree.

I think it was late fall, because the sun lit through objects as if they were composed of water. Around this time the masses of dragonflies were starting to disappear, and, bored with the hunt, I went to this park often. It was the perfect place to while away an empty day. People who had nothing to do and less in their pockets were scattered here and there in the park like used tissues. Bored and hungry, I killed time watching the chess gamblers, dart throwers, people playing simplified chess, and the fighters in the fighting ring.

A vendor always sat on the first stone step at the entrance of the park. I don't think she ever changed her spot. She always looked the same, with a towel neatly wrapped around the traditional bun at the back of her head. Nothing ever changed, not the old newspapers on the ground, the small pile of nicked apples on top, or her indifferent eyes that waited for customers. She always sat in front of her wares like that. But that wasn't why I noticed her. Other vendors were there with their goods spread out as well. It was her strange habits that forced me to look at her.

Even at a glance, her products were inferior. The apples were so marred and rotten that if this were the countryside where they had been harvested, they would have been swept into a pig's trough. Even though we were going through a food shortage and her goods were dirt cheap, I thought it was shameful to try to sell that kind of fruit.

But she was unruffled. She sat there innocently for hours, expressionless as an idiot, the almost inedible apples piled up in front of her. Even though it wasn't the season, flies buzzed around her display. It must have been a splendid meal for them. She didn't chase away the flies that persistently attached themselves to the apples. They were left alone, as if she had prepared this display for them. It was quite a generous offering.

Then again, they were the only ones interested in her products. I never saw anyone buy even one apple from her. Even the rare few who looked in her direction turned quickly away, perplexed. She didn't seem disappointed. She only smiled briefly like an idiot.

Her strange habits started after that. She picked up an apple, as if she had forgotten that they were there. With a long, dry finger resembling a chopstick, she dug out the parts on which the flies had been feasting, and brought the morsels to her mouth. She acted like they were precious bites and ate slowly, just like snacking children. After she finished burrowing out only the rotten parts, she started on another apple.

I don't know why she reminded me of Mother. Though desolate, the sunlight shining down on the park was as light and lucid as my empty stomach. Even though it was the same autumn sunlight, the light enveloping my neighborhood was dry and gray. Returning home, having failed to spend the whole day at the park, I saw gloomy sheets of light hanging here and there in the narrow and muddy alleys. I imagined the woman putting her large tray on her head and leaving the park. I visualized her stomach, filled with pieces of rotten apple. At least she wouldn't go hungry.

The day, through which I suffered with pangs of hunger, was finally over.

A Single Rotten Apple

Not everyone in our neighborhood was poor. Mr. Gwak, the secondhand dealer, Mr. Han, who ran one of the shops clustered in the Yankee market, and Mr. Choe, the head of the neighborhood association, whose wife exchanged dollars, were known to be well off. I'm not sure if they really were hiding stiff new bills somewhere in their box-like rooms. But everyone believed it to be true. From what I could gather, a few more could be counted among the affluent. Mr. Kim, suffering from the A-bomb disease, was one.

Mr. Kim was a victim of a bigger war. A tall man with large eyes, he apparently crossed the borders of three or four countries—including his own—as if he were hopping over a woven millet-stalk fence. He was in Hiroshima (or perhaps Nagasaki) during the last days of the gale-like violence. It was August 6th (or perhaps it was the 9th) of that nightmarish year. It was a clear day. An airplane was high in the sky, its silver wings flashing. It was a B-29. The smoke coming out of the tail split the sky neatly in half. That was it. It cut such a clear and beautiful picture that it was hard to believe it was wartime. Mr. Kim said that he thought of his hometown,

remembering the moment that he was saddened by a lost kite as a
boy. At that instant, a gigantic flash of light and noise, never before
experienced by anyone, tore apart the picture.

When he opened his eyes—he repeated this part many times—
he was struck with the premonition that he would never again be
able to stand. Unfortunately, his prediction came true. He was bedridden, his condition weighing his heart down like cancer. If you
looked into Mr. Kim's room, you could see him lying there as if
asleep, propped up by pillows. People said that he often revisited
the scene of the explosion in his sleep. We heard his screams from
time to time. For him, the great war was unending. Sometimes, in
the middle of the day, the silver wings of the B-29 would float on
the ceiling of his box-like room, and then the thousandth A-bomb
would again shatter his small world.

"This damn world! Who's tougher, you or me?"

Mr. Kim always uttered these words when his hurricane of a
nightmare passed. Sometimes he sang a foreign song in a tired voice,
and each time I heard it, I would feel the cold death spreading slowly
from the tips of his toes to his heart.

"*Saraba hiroshimayo madaguru madewa . . .*"

Neither America the winner nor Japan the defeated supported
the war-wounded Mr. Kim. Of course, nor did his own impov-
erished country. Mr. Kim had a loyal brother, who had become
quite a successful businessman in Japan after moving there empty-
handed. He was the one supporting Mr. Kim, who had been ruined by the crazed war. That was why Mr. Kim was one of the
richer men in our neighborhood. His neighbors envied him, saying that more money than could be spent came across the ocean,

enabling him to live comfortably. They were so envious of his brother that they were even jealous of the fact that he had been struck by the A-bomb.

"I'd be glad to be hit by a bigger A-bomb, if only I were able to lie around," my neighbors often said, a complaint revealing that the difficulties of living weren't any less than dealing with the A-bomb disease. I suppose I agreed with this sentiment a little. Even though Mr. Kim depended on his wife for everything except for tasting and digesting food, he always had something to snack on, from rock candy to *senbei* cookies, from squid legs to a bottle of refined rice wine. His kids were always eating something too, making my unhappiness that much more acute.

Referring to the Kims' kids, the neighbors often joked that Mr. Kim could still perform. It was a mystery if you took their kids' ages into account. Some thought it had to do with Mrs. Kim's personality, as outgoing as any man's, and others would pointlessly discuss the scientific possibilities. Mr. Gwak and Mr. Choe, Mr. Kim's drinking and conversation buddies, visited him often. Listening to their talk from the outside, I would be tricked into thinking that Mr. Kim was sitting up and moving around like a normal person. Once, I overheard their conversation:

"Be honest. Who's sowing the oats at night?" Mr. Gwak asked. "It's just so amazing. Do you have a secret method?"

Mrs. Kim said with a short laugh, "Why? Do you think he's hiring a day laborer?"

A torrent of laughter burst forth. The Kims laughed the loudest and the heartiest. Mr. Kim's laughter was especially impressive. It allowed me to glimpse his free younger days.

"You sound like you want to be a part of the workforce," Mr. Kim said, laughing.

Mr. Choe, who had been laughing till then, added, "I guess Gwak's income isn't so great these days."

There was another big burst of merriment.

At the very least, Mr. Kim wasn't lonely. Even though he was immobile and his world was limited to the rectangular box-like room, Mr. Kim's life revealed his generous, down-to-earth personality. Compared to his, Mother's world was lonely and sad. I would sit near her, who only had an empty water bowl nearby. Her breathing was labored. Even though she had often been ill, she had never been confined to bed before. She lay in bed that entire lonely autumn, as if getting out of bed would mean she were giving up on Father.

Mrs. Kim came to our room with a man in a white coat.

"Now, sit up," she said, helping Mother up. She said, unsparingly, "I can't stand looking at people sick in bed."

The man in the white coat was a doctor. He came to check on Mr. Kim once a month. I assumed that he had come over on Mrs. Kim's request after examining his patient.

"Let's get you examined, just to see what's wrong. You can't lie in bed like this every day," Mrs. Kim said as if coaxing a stubborn child, and the man in the white coat looked around the room before opening his bag. His face was white and soft, like a woman's. I decided that all doctors look like him, with similar complexions. I thought I would be able to guess what he did for a living even if he didn't have the white coat on or carry the black bag.

Mother was very shy. That was inevitable—I think it was her first and only examination. The prognosis shocked us. Mrs. Kim was so flabbergasted that she giggled. But Mother was very calm. She didn't look surprised, even though she blushed a bit.

"The problem is that the mother's body is too weak," the doctor said. "It's hard to expect a normal birth at this point. But it's too late to do anything. Your health is a problem, and it will be more at risk as the fetus grows. Be brave. You need to be healthier, no matter what."

Our room seemed even emptier when Mrs. Kim and the doctor left. Mother lay back down, and Sister and I sat near her silently. We didn't turn on the light even when darkness slowly filled our room. Mother was looking at the wall. Sister stared at the floor. I couldn't figure out what she was thinking. Even in the dark, I could sense the small smile flitting across my sister's lips.

My thoughts were mixed up. I couldn't think straight for a while. I thought about Mr. Kim and his A-bomb story, Mrs. Kim and their kids, and my absent father and Mother's pregnancy. My head felt as if it would burst, but I still couldn't single out a feeling. I thought again of the doctor, his clear, white, woman-like complexion, and his words.

Mrs. Kim dropped in again. She had ordered black-bean noodles for her kids. She gave us a bowl as well. Mother sat up and forced herself to take a few bites. Greedily sharing the leftover noodles with Sister, I remembered the woman in the park with her rotten apples. I don't know why I thought of her at that moment. My throat closed up with the food I had stuffed into my mouth.

Mother had only had water. But something like a rotten apple was growing in her stomach. I hiccupped violently.

Tofu Flesh

She was about two years older than Sister. I can't remember whether her name was Yeong-ja or Jeong-ja. I only remember her big physique and glowing skin. If you didn't take her age or heft into consideration, her body was that of a chubby baby. People said it was because she ate a lot of tofu. Tofu was the most nutritious food we knew of. We couldn't imagine a more nutritious food than that, other than eggs or whale meat. I'm not sure how accurate this was, but we all believed that even President Syngman Rhee, worried about malnourished citizens after the war, actively encouraged the distribution of tofu.

People called Sister's friend Tofu Flesh. She was lucky—her father ran the only tofu factory in the neighborhood. Though only a small-scale home production, they made enough that they didn't have to limit their only daughter's intake. Through the winter fog-like steam in her house, you could see her father and her four grown brothers sweating and vigorously grinding beans in a stone mill, and the finished tofu immersed in a large water tank. One brother died in the war and another had lost his leg. But still, she was one of the lucky ones in our shantytown. I knew that from the tofu-filled wooden trays stacked around her. It was obvious why she was so healthy, with soft, white, tofu-like skin.

Tofu Flesh was Sister's friend. Or maybe Sister was Tofu Flesh's friend. I'm not sure who offered her friendship first, but she was Sister's sole friend. Tofu Flesh, on the other hand, had many more friends other than Sister, and from what I understood, even had boyfriends. She was able to make friends freely thanks to her age, health, and most importantly, her comfortable upbringing. If you took these into account, Sister was merely one of Tofu Flesh's many friends.

One day Sister didn't come home till late. It had never happened before. Mother didn't say anything. She just lay there like a crumpled sack. Waiting for Sister fell solely on me. It was a very lonely and boring task, but I decided to be patient. It would be worth waiting up for her if she had gone out with Tofu Flesh.

It was worth it. When she came home, Sister, as if providing an alibi for her whereabouts, cautiously unwrapped something. It was obvious: Sister had been at Tofu Flesh's house this whole time. What other detail could Mother have asked for? The chunk of tofu on a plate and the large amount of soy pulp clearly proved her innocence. Not understanding what was going on, I almost whooped like a small child in front of a food-laden table. Mother quietly sat up. She said only one thing, which stopped me from greedily attacking the food.

"Go throw it out."

I couldn't sleep. I realized afresh that you couldn't sleep well if your stomach was empty. I looked around. I could see Sister's open eyes in the dark. She looked lost in thought.

I whispered in her ear, "Were you really at their house all this time?"

She nodded in the dark.

"Do you think Tofu Flesh is a good friend?"

She didn't say anything. After a long pause, I asked, "Are you going there again tomorrow?"

"No," she said definitively, "Mother probably won't let me."

I still couldn't fall asleep. We lay there, staring at each other for a long time. We could hear our tired neighbors snore; they were so noisy that they could have brought down the walls.

The next morning, Tofu Flesh came to our house accompanied by a woman. I instantly figured out who she was: her mother. She was a bit fat, but had soft white skin like her daughter. *It's thanks to all that tofu*, I thought when they came into our room and sat down. The room seemed to burst at the seams. It was the first time we'd met her. Mother finally sat up, her expression stiff and cold. I was worried that she might turn our guests away. Sister must have been thinking the same thing. Her eyes, looking at the two mothers, were nervous.

Thankfully, the meeting between the two women ended quickly. Tofu Flesh's mother was as magnanimous as she looked and Mother had no reason to hide her true feelings, so their conversation was succinct. Tofu Flesh's mother asked what Mother thought of sending Sister off to live with them, and Mother replied that she didn't even want to think about it. Then, when Tofu Flesh's mother said that she wasn't planning to rob her of her precious daughter so just consider it, Mother said that she would rather eat dirt than have to contemplate that kind of transaction. Since the back-and-forths were like that, a transaction could hardly happen. Soon, thorns sprouted on their words and thin ice formed.

"I'm not saying this just because I'm rather better off. I'm only mentioning it because she is so gentle and nice that I want her for one of my sons. Aren't all mothers of sons like-minded?" Tofu Flesh's mother said, quite sharply. As if she were scolding Mother for being dim-witted, she added, "Even if they are your children, you have to feed them and clothe them first. Think about it carefully. It would be better if you sent her to us as a future daughter-in-law instead of starving them like this."

Mother didn't say anything to these words, which, even to my young heart, felt a little like an insult. Only Sister blushed. Tofu Flesh smiled the whole time, not caring where the conversation was going. Seeing how relaxed Tofu Flesh was, I wondered whether their family had come to an agreement with my sister.

After they left, I thought about Tofu Flesh's four brothers. I felt very strange thinking that one of them could be my future brother-in-law. But it was clear that I didn't have a say in the issue. I just hoped that he wouldn't be the one without a leg.

Uncle

Early one morning, Mother unexpectedly started moving about. Even though this had been our biggest wish, I was worried that something was wrong.

First, Mother cleaned our room, and then the outside. She washed her hair and wound it into a neat bun. Her movements, unlike those of someone who had gotten up after a long illness, were alert and peaceful.

She hesitated in front of the small but well-polished old-fashioned chest in the corner of the room. In it was a neat stack of our clothing. Not a single breast-tie or a sleeve poked out from the stack, a reflection of her orderly personality.

It was that time of year when even the noon sun seemed weak. I thought Mother was looking over our winter clothes. She took out a couple of outfits from the depths of the chest. After studying them for a long while, she finally chose one and put it on. It was the soft silk top and skirt she had worn whenever she went to the town market, held every fifth day, before we moved to this ludicrous city. I felt a vague sorrow when she stood up wearing the light blue outfit. I realized how serious her illness was—it was more advanced than we had imagined.

"Follow me," Mother said to me in a low voice. The morning sun brightened the narrow alley lined with wood shacks.

We arrived at Uncle's house around lunchtime. After getting off the bus, we walked 10 *ri*. It took two hours. The fall harvest was under way in the fields. The various sights gave me a feeling of abundance. Mother was very tired. She stopped to rest often, and each time she cast an indifferent glance over the autumn fields. I couldn't tell what she was thinking.

Uncle was one of Mother's stepsiblings. I didn't know anything about him, other than that he had lost an arm in the war. If there hadn't been a war, or if he had come out of it untouched, I wouldn't have even known that he was my uncle.

I didn't get a good first impression of him. He gave off a certain cold and creepy feeling, the way you might feel if you encountered a still working rusted gun with small broken parts. He was a man of few words. He barely said anything to me even though it was the first time he had met his nephew. That afternoon, he spoke only a couple of times, to criticize Father's incompetence.

"Do you think people are easy on me because I'm crippled? Do you think I got some medal for it? There isn't a single asshole who looks at me when I go around the marketplace like this. Even I can survive, so what kind of normal man goes and gets himself shackled for transporting something stolen?"

Mother didn't say anything. She sat there hunched, her head bowed, listening quietly. She must have made up her mind when she left home to remain firm in the face of humiliation. Her neat bun and the straight part in her hair revealed her unwavering decision. I was annoyed. Why did Mother come to this good-for-nothing uncle, especially when she was unwell? I kept tugging on her skirt.

We returned home late. Exhausted, we fell into bed. The next morning, eating white rice for the first time in a long while, the inside of my mouth felt unpleasant. Sitting with my family at the table, I recalled Uncle's unwelcoming expression. But I'd be happy to see him one more time for a reward like this. After gulping down my portion, I ran outside eagerly. I thought something exciting might happen that day. There were a lot of kids in the alley, looking happier and cleaner than usual. A few boys exploded paper bombs and several girls seesawed on a washboard.

I felt numb. I couldn't join them right away for some reason. Some dim memory was lurking at the edge of my consciousness. A very exciting, important memory . . .

Sister, who had come to stand behind me, said in a very small and sad voice, "It's Harvest Moon Festival today . . ."

I finally understood the scene in front of me. I nodded dumbly, subdued before I got a chance to have some fun.

Jail Visit

I'm not sure if it was the Rose of Sharon brand or the Bear brand. I just remember that the flour wasn't of high quality judging from its slight reddish-black color. Anyway, Mr. Choe brought us a sack. He said that even though it was a bit late, this was government-issue relief for the destitute in time for Harvest Moon Festival. We had no idea if that was really the case.

Mr. Choe was a very good neighborhood head, since he looked out for the residents. He had been a table-tennis player in school and had won several municipal and provincial competitions. Compared to his taller-than-average wife, an active trader exchanging won for American dollars, he was a small man with a girlish face. If I borrowed Mr. Gwak's description, the couple resembled a fly sitting on a kettle lid.

"Mr. Choe, you shouldn't ever let your wife get on top even in the most urgent situation. I'm always afraid that I might have to help her with your funeral expenses," Mr. Gwak often said, laughing.

Thanks to his kettle lid-like wife, Mr. Choe led a leisurely life like that of a summer fly. But he never wasted his time. He bustled around for his neighbors. Everyone said it would be fitting if all the residents of the shantytown erected a monument in his honor for his distinguished services.

But Mr. Choe hadn't come to our house just to give us a sack of flour. Brushing off the flour from his hands, Mr. Choe said to Mother, "I think I'm going to pay him a visit. It looks like he's going to be sentenced and transferred, and then it will be hard to visit him. I think this might be the last visit, so it would be nice if you could come too."

I understood what this was about. Mother remained silent, her sickly face pointing downward.

Mr. Choe spoke again. "No, of course you shouldn't overtax yourself. That won't benefit anyone. I'll just go visit him by myself."

Mother still didn't say anything. She just ducked her head lower. I was filled with desperation. Probably because it showed on my face, Mr. Choe, who had been about to leave, peered into my eyes. A hot arrow pierced my small heart.

"Would it be all right to take him?" Mr. Choe asked.

I finally realized what I had been wishing for. I stared at Mother's lips impatiently. She didn't say anything, but we understood her thoughts. I followed Mr. Choe out without hesitation.

The jail was situated between the courthouse and City Hall. It took less than an hour to get there. I hadn't even imagined that Father had been so near. I felt as if I had been cheated all along. I had been foolish, thinking that Father was somewhere far, far away. I regretted that I hadn't come earlier.

The jailhouse seemed to have a long history. I hadn't seen such an old and depressing building in the city before. I saw door-less walls, ash-colored roofs, and the broken skyline. I felt confined. I couldn't believe that a person could breathe, move, and be kept in such a place. I especially couldn't imagine that Father had lived here till now.

We had to wait a few hours to meet Father. I sat on a wooden chair in the crowded waiting room during that tedious time. It would have looked like a waiting room in a small train station if it weren't so dark and depressed. It was as if the train everyone was waiting for had already come and gone, or as if it would never get there. I could read on their faces a bigger despair than waiting.

We were able to see him after a long wait. Father hadn't changed much. He looked the same as usual, except for his unruly beard and strange-looking jail uniform. I felt deflated. Father was the same as when he used to traverse the alley on his rattling secondhand bicycle. I felt as if he would laugh at me. Of course, he didn't. Instead, he looked extremely embarrassed. Standing awkwardly on the other side of the steel barrier dividing the visiting room in half, he smiled very uncomfortably. This smile was one thing I found to be new. I couldn't forget that absurd, even dimwitted, smile even after returning home. It is possible that Father hadn't fully grasped his newly restricted life.

A flock of pigeons pecked at overgrown weeds in the yard in front of the visiting room. An old couple walked a few steps ahead of Mr. Choe and me, their footsteps as hollow as the wind. I suddenly heard the city's noise, squeezed into a tight space. I felt uncomfortable and strange. People talking, cars honking, and all kinds of other noises weighed heavily on my empty heart. I thought of Mother and Sister. I suddenly missed them instead of Father.

Gleaning

Sometimes when I walked out into the alley early in the morning, white frost would be blanketing the ground. Other times, columns of frost as sharp as blades sprouted up overnight. It was a sign that winter was coming slowly to the city, to our poor neighborhood.

My friends and I left the neighborhood, stepping through the frost. Morning sunlight was the freshest. The alleys and the roofs, patched with pieces of cans and pasteboard, shimmered like silver fish. Small, shiny crystals broke apart under our feet. Tiny, pristine icicles, looking like needles or pillars, or sometimes like wide sheets or cups, felt good on our skins. We could feel the season's chill as clearly as the goose bumps prickling up through our skin.

The morning market was almost over. All sorts of fruits and vegetables from nearby farms had already reached the final retailer. The merchandise, heaped around the market, was distributed among bicycles, wooden carts, and buckets destined to be sent all over the city. By early morning, the wholesale market was empty, like a beach at low tide. We started our work when the retailers slung their fat money purses around their waists, brushed off their hands, and left the market to eat hearty beef soup.

We were here to glean in the city. As we had done in the fields after the fall harvest, we looked for scraps in the shuttered market. We didn't expect to find much. But on lucky days, those filled with transactions, Sister and I would find two or three armfuls of greens, though rotten or mashed. But this was rare, and most mornings we would find very little.

The market wasn't that big. You could pass through it in ten minutes even at busy times. Divided into many groups, we kids usually spent two hours, sometimes even three or four, searching like starving rat packs.

"I guess the market's already over, since those damn kids are poking around everywhere," the occasional late-arriving merchants would grumble, turning back empty-handed.

Our group split naturally into two, and each scavenged the market from opposite ends. As a strategy, Sister and I split up as well. She started from the entrance of the market, while I searched from the inside toward her. Inevitably, we met in the middle after about an hour. As always, I quickly checked Sister's basket. There were twenty-odd potatoes as small as birds' eggs and a few tough cabbage leaves. I thought she had found more than usual. I had less, only a sack of radish leaves.

"Well, you have a lot more in volume," Sister offered, wiping away the sweat glistening on her nose. I smiled awkwardly.

"We should get back home," she said, walking ahead of me. "We searched so much that the ground is clean."

I followed her quietly. The market was messy, filled with the garbage we had scattered. Only the cleaners would take the remaining scraps. We had taken every last bit that could be eaten.

"We should stop coming here," Sister said suddenly.

"Why?"

"Well . . . I just think we should."

A couple of kids from our group were clustered in front of the market. I realized we were in trouble as soon as I saw their expressions. I saw a market caretaker with an armband roughly grabbing the front of a kid's shirt.

"That kid stole something!" whispered a boy urgently, his voice trembling with strange excitement.

My heart froze.

"Let me see it, or you'll get a beating!" insisted the caretaker, letting go of the kid. Finally, the kid dumped the contents of his sack on the ground, perhaps thinking that there was no other way out. Several fresh, healthy radishes rolled out.

"That son of a bitch! I knew it. He stole two zucchinis yesterday," angrily mumbled the boy who had been whispering in my ear.

The caretaker inspected all of us. The results made him even angrier. A few other kids had committed the same crime. I don't think the stolen items amounted to very much, and I believe that a few of us were innocent. But even if we had only taken a piece of fruit or a bunch of greens, we weren't in the position to defend ourselves. The ones who had been fortunate in the morning gleaning paid for their luck with a slap from the caretaker.

But the thing that humiliated us the most wasn't the stealing or even getting slapped. We were taken aback by the fact that the food we'd gathered, spilled into the street for everyone to see, was so pitiful. I grew embarrassed; we had woken up so early to gather such a meager heap.

Preoccupied, Sister hurriedly swept up the vegetables spilled on the ground as if she were being chased. I stared blankly down at her red, frostbitten hands. Something like raindrops splashed on them. I looked up at the sky, dyed gold by the morning sunlight.

Silkworms

Father's sister came to our house. She was the first relative to visit us since our move.

I bumped into her in the alley when the sun was about to set. It was also the time of day when I felt my hunger the most. I knew from experience that it would become easier to withstand it if I got over this crucial moment. In the evening, I would feel a slight dizziness instead of pain. I would pour a bowl of cold water into my empty stomach, and then the dizziness would go away completely. The emptier my stomach, the cleaner and clearer my head. If nothing out of the ordinary happened, I would go to bed with a lucid consciousness. How could I have dreamed of a surprise visit from Auntie?

I was squatting in front of a plank wall, looking up at the sun, when she stopped in front of me. I looked slowly at the intruder.

"Yun," she said, looking down at me. "Do you know who I am?"

I thought she looked familiar. Her face was as thin as a piece of firewood and she had a long, straight nose. It was a dead-ringer for a man's nose—no, Father's nose.

I finally recognized her. She had married and lost her husband earlier than her peers, becoming one of many war widows. I remembered their wedding feast that took place a year or two before the war. Even though I was still able to withstand my hunger, that faint memory made me dizzy.

—

I remember looking at the guests crowding the narrow country road and the single path through the field. A tent swayed in our yard, and the entire village was in a festive mood. Grandmother fed me liquor. "If you've come into the world with a pepper, you should know how to drink a cup or two of liquor, even if you don't become a great drinker. It won't do if you can't drink, like your father and grandfather . . ."

An entire group of people laughed. It was an overflowing laughter, much like the food at the party. I gulped down the liquor boldly and ended up in tears, rolling around on the straw mat. The memory of that day's dizziness, or rather that day's satiety, made my empty stomach lurch.

Anyway, that's how Auntie got married. And that winter, soon after the war broke out, she became a widow, while many of her contemporaries were still single.

—

I stood up silently. My legs were asleep. I scuffed toward our room without saying anything to Auntie.

Sister's and Mother's welcomes were similarly cold. Nobody greeted her warmly. Poor Auntie was so upset that she started to sob as soon as she entered the room. Sitting in a heap near Mother, she cried harder than she had when she'd lost her husband.

Mother was lying down, facing the wall, but she couldn't hide her sorrow. Her skeletal shoulders shook violently. Sister couldn't hold back either. Burying her face in Auntie's hunched back, she leaked, little by little, very small, hard sobs. The crying was so intense that Mrs. Kim ran in to see what the matter was.

My eyes prickled and my chest squeezed as if my diaphragm would break in half, but I couldn't cry. What are tears? It's merely the act of releasing something that is crammed in your body. I couldn't release anything from my small body. So nobody can criticize me for having failed to join in on their sadness.

Of the several presents Auntie brought, the silkworms made me the happiest. Quite a lot of those brown bugs were in a large nickel container. Oh, how they were cute! With wonder, I studied their shiny dark brown bodies, their deep, compact wrinkles, and their wavy, regularly spaced lines, squashed like small tree rings. Saliva pooled in my mouth. How could she have picked only the cutest, tastiest, cleanest ones to fill an entire container? I decided that Auntie was a great woman. She went back the same day, leaving behind a rough sketch of a map to her workplace. Sister and I planned to visit her the following noon. But we made it there two days later, because we had greedily eaten too much of her wondrous present and had gotten upset stomachs.

Auntie worked at a huge raw silk factory. She took us to see a spinner. Everything within sight was novel to us. Every single thing amazed us—the machines lined up neatly as if drawn with a ruler, the female workers, the kilns as big as nickel pots, the spools of silk thread, the silkworms shaped like peanuts, tiny balls, squares, or sometimes ovals. Auntie took out some salt from her lunch box. We had forgotten we were hungry. Following her instructions, we took out the silkworms carefully from the kilns and ate them. It was strangely delicious. Scooped out of the boiling water, the brown bugs were hot and soft. I couldn't think of anything, even an expensive made-to-order dish, that would be more delicious or more nutritious. Sister and I ate quickly.

Heading home with a silkworm-filled nickel container wrapped in nylon cloth, I said sleepily to Sister, "I wish you worked at a factory like this. Then we could eat silkworms every day!"

I'm sure Sister couldn't imagine anything better at that moment either. With ardent hope-filled eyes, she looked behind her. I did the same and saw Auntie standing motionless in front of the guard post.

Our Feast

Mother became paler and more transparent with every passing day. It wasn't just her face. Her hands and ankles, peeking out from under the blanket, looked the same. Thread-like veins were visible under her pale skin. The transformation of her appearance was so expected that it didn't even surprise me. Mother didn't want to eat anything other than, once in a very long while, a few sips of water. It was logical that her body would become as transparent as cast-off snakeskin. Looking at Mother lying in bed like a dead woman, facing the wall, I would fantasize often. In this eye-blinding fantasy, she would finally cast off her worn body and fly up to the heavens like a butterfly or dragonfly, brightly illuminated by the sun.

We couldn't receive anything from the Protestant church. Their supplies had dwindled as soon as winter came. We rushed over every Sunday, remembering the dry, mouth-filling taste of powdered milk, but returned home empty-handed each time.

It was the same at the Catholic church. We only got a few pieces of clothing at the end of the year. We gave up that trip regretfully, thinking that God had run out of supplies as well. But we couldn't deny that their clothes helped us through the winter. Though secondhand, the clothes shielded us from the cold a little. But even the best winter clothes couldn't block out the iciness generated from our insides. The chill we felt from being hungry was severer. Our hunger was a little easier to deal with if we bundled up in winter clothes. But only a little. And we had the equivalent amount of piety left in us.

Of course, some kids were exceptions. That girl who'd had a seizure was one. We all knew that her father had been a devout Christian on the other side of the 38th Parallel. But she hadn't brought her piety from the North, because she'd frequented the Protestant church on the hill and the Catholic church downtown like the rest of us. She hadn't wanted to give up either the small amount of powdered milk or the two scoops of cornmeal.

There had been a turning point for her. Her father, who pulled a cart in a transport company's warehouse, had hurt his back badly and become bedridden. Her attitude changed with her father's misfortune. She became very devout, as if her religiosity propped her father up. She went to the tented church on that windy hill every morning. Still pale and weak, she didn't wear long underwear even in the middle of winter, saying that her faith helped her forget the cold. Whenever she saw one of the kids roaming around hungry, she would say, "Pray hard. Did you know that if you pray hard, you forget that you're hungry? My father said that you shouldn't live on bread, but on God's words. People who believe don't get hungry."

I could vividly imagine how the poor father and daughter withstood their hunger. I thought that the sickly girl would collapse next to her father sooner or later. But surprisingly, she got through the winter. I don't know what happened to them in the end, but at least one thing is definite. The weak, sickly girl was hanging on, undefeated, when my family left the shantytown. I can't think of her small, pale face, especially her cavernous eyes, without a stab of pain in my heart. Many years later, I was surprised to find similar eyes on refugee children from Biafra. But their eyes weren't burning and shiny, like hers.

I must confess that I was gradually attracted to that girl. My small heart kept leaning toward her, first because of her shocking seizure, then because of her sickly appearance, and finally because of her moving faith. I lingered around her at church, in the streets, and even in my dreams.

Her words weren't false. I was sometimes able to satisfy my hunger for a while by picturing her face. Of course, those instances were very brief. But I was able to understand how she could forget her hunger by thinking of, and praying to, God. Even though I didn't know much, I realized that you would probably see more results by thinking of God instead of the girl. One evening when I was hungrier than most days, I crept up to the church on the hill. Thankfully, our Sunday school tent was empty. I felt uneasy, but a more desperate emotion—pain, the pain of a starving body—propelled me. I knelt on the wooden floor and clasped my hands together. The result was very embarrassing. It would have been better to pray to the girl. I couldn't stay there because of my gut-wrenching hunger. Ashamed and feeling empty, I ran out. I was shaking all over. I trembled so severely that I felt cold sweat seeping out of me. Walking sideways down the windy hill, I gave everybody the finger.

—

"Drink some water," Sister said calmly. She handed me the water bowl sitting by Mother. I took in a mouthful. It was very cold. I took another sip, shivering. I felt better. I could feel the water going down my gullet and gliding softly into my empty stomach. I felt refreshed.

"You'll get sick if you drink it too quickly." Sister took the water bowl and slowly took a sip. I took it back and drank slowly, as if I were savoring its taste, as Sister had.

Mother was wiser than the girl. Water had all sorts of tastes. It didn't only taste good. I could substitute it with the colors and shapes of all the foods I could ever imagine. Drinking water allowed for a big fantasy feast. Wrapped in blankets, Sister and I sat facing each other and took turns drinking the water, no, enjoying the feast. And it satisfied us. Sleep by way of heavy drowsiness came upon us.

Prisoners

At dawn, I awoke from a fitful sleep. I realized that we had hit some kind of unclimbable wall. Hunger. It was the first truly cold day of that winter. As soon as I opened my eyes, I was faced with a wall standing firmly in front of me, blocking my view. I couldn't look the other way any longer. I felt strangely calm. *It's such an obvious solution.* There were only two ways to conquer the wall. I already knew which one I had to choose.

Still in bed, I looked around the room slowly. Every surface was covered in white frost, except for the floor. Mother and Sister were still asleep. They were deep in a cold and hungry sleep, their backs hunched like shrimp.

I stepped outside quietly. The first snow of the year cozily blanketed the shantytown. People said that, on snowy days, beggars bundled up under the eaves and picked lice out of their ragged clothes. Actually, it felt warmer than the night before.

I found a military mess kit lying around in the kitchen. The tin bucket was big enough for my purposes. I left, my wool hat pulled down to my eyes. I didn't go out of my way to hide from the neighbors' eyes. But, in a stroke of luck, I didn't bump into anyone until I emerged from the snow-covered alley. I was emboldened. Returning from a day of begging for food, I couldn't expect that kind of fortune. Even though the snow kept falling, adding to the ankle-deep drifts, the residents had to go out and be resourceful. I had no choice but to be seen. There was even a group of kids engaged in a riotous snowball fight in the narrow alley. The tin bucket was hefty and I didn't even try to hide it. The only thing I could do when I encountered someone I knew was to pull my hat down lower over my eyes and look down at my feet.

Events unfolded as I had expected. Sister would have been less reluctant to touch a snake. Of course, she didn't say anything to Mother. It was a hard struggle between us, an intense but silent fight. What would I have done with that damn tin bucket if Sister hadn't caved in? It would have been terrible if I had to throw out the contents of the bucket or if I had to leave the house again with it. Our fight didn't end easily. Her head bowed, Sister seemed too ashamed to even look at me. Her face was bright red. I felt as if I were going to burst. My humiliating act of begging wasn't Sister's only opponent. She was engaged in a deadly silent battle with the world, and with herself.

The price we paid for sating our hunger wasn't small. We couldn't leave our room that entire day. We didn't move an inch, even though the soft, gentle snowflakes outside beckoned. Balled up in the small space, I thought of Father. The father who sold his conscience and the son who rid himself of his pride were one and the same—prisoners.

Starving Soul

One day, both fortunate and unfortunate things happened to me, taking turns. They arrived one after another, as if they had been arranged beforehand, surprising me each time. It was the kind of day that could have crammed the highlights of your entire life into twenty-four hours.

Fortune came first. I was able to fill my mess kit without going to very many houses. This was an anomaly. I sometimes had to sweep a neighborhood two kilometers away to fill a two-liter mess kit. In those days, people locked the gate during mealtimes even if they left it open overnight. It wasn't something to fault or blame. That was just the way people survived in the destitute '50s. Everyone was poor. Since there wasn't anything for a thief to take, there was no need to lock the doors. But people weren't pitiless enough to withhold a morsel of food. Even today, I don't resent those who had to lock their soft hearts.

Sometimes my kit would be empty, even after I circled half of the city. You couldn't get rid of pride with one transaction. Like water refilling an empty spring, my pride never went away, which hindered me. I could only be a clumsy and embarrassed pilgrim. I always wished that the kit would fill as soon as possible, so that I could make fewer pilgrimages.

My fortune wasn't a small one. I checked the amount, which was satisfactory. We would be able to eat for three days. The kit contained more than five different grains. It looked like I had collected samples of all kinds of harvestable grains in my mess kit. I was able to discern the different kinds because I was still a hick, who had been playing in the countryside only a year ago. I poked through the contents with my finger. Rice, barley, wheat, sorghum, Chinese millet, glutinous millet, regular millet, kidney beans, *mame* beans, peas, mung beans, red beans, yellow beans, chestnuts, castor beans, pressed barley, fluffy Vietnamese rice . . . I finally grasped the source of my fortune. It wasn't pure luck, but rather the result of the festive morning of the year's first full moon.

Just at that moment, misfortune caught up with me. It pounced on me suddenly, the way these things often do. I was knocked off my feet. I had no idea what hit me. It crashed into me so forcefully that I couldn't gather my thoughts for a while. I recognized what had happened a little later. Lying on the ground, I stared at it. The disaster—my attacker—was in the form of a German shepherd. The beast glared at me, its red tongue hanging out. Fear shot down my spine. I didn't budge. I thought it would attack me again if I lifted even a finger.

A middle-aged man ran out, aghast. His face was tense, and he looked more shocked than I was. I relaxed. It wasn't a big deal after all. The furry ball of disaster went back into its house obediently. Instead of baring its sharp teeth, it cravenly wagged its tail, courting its owner's favor. Seeing that angered me. I couldn't lie there any longer like a loser. I stood up lightly, brushing myself off. A quick electric current shot down my left leg, but it wasn't too bad. The bigger pain I felt wasn't physical. Standing up awkwardly, I stared down at the ground. My empty mess kit rolled near my feet, its contents scattered on the frozen ground. I slowly realized how wretched my tragedy was. My entire shameful universe had spilled onto the ground.

But I soon recovered with the arrival of another fortune. The middle-aged man was the bearer of good news. He had completely regained his calm by now, despite his initial fright. I told him that my wound wasn't serious, and he didn't bother to check whether I was telling the truth. Instead, he said a few reassuring words and told me to be careful. He offered to refill my empty mess kit, but I firmly refused. I don't know why I did. He searched through his pockets, took out a few bills, and gave them to me. Obtaining cash was more than garden-variety luck. I couldn't think about anything else. I stood there like an idiot, feeling as if I'd been caught by a searchlight, staring at the gates locked securely behind the man. It was definitely a lucky thing. But somehow, it didn't seem real. I opened my fist cautiously. They were still there. My second fortune of the day had taken the form of three old, tattered bills. I quickly curled my fingers over them. I was anxious, thinking that my luck would change again and fly away like a bird. I shoved my fist deep into my pocket and hurried away as if I were a fugitive.

First, I bought myself a bun stuffed with red beans shaped like a fat fish, with a yellowish back and a spongy stomach. I will never forget the sweetness, warmth, and softness I felt when I bit into the tail. Nothing is more exact than one's tongue. I verified my luck with my clever tongue, not with my empty heart, and thought it would be safe to believe my fortune. I handed over a bill and got a lot of change in return. I hid the coins in my pocket. I walked around, wanting to whistle, my hand stuck in the depths of my pocket. Through my fingertips, I could hear the constant happy chatter of the two mother bills and a number of baby coins.

So many things beckoned me in the streets. Chinese pancakes, roasted sweet potatoes, fishcakes, spicy rice cakes, peanuts, *senbei* cookies, white taffy, round buns, unhatched old eggs . . . Seeing no reason to hesitate, I stopped often. I had been starved for so long, and a fortune jingled in my pocket, a fortune that couldn't be more real.

There were many other things in the market where I used to glean leftover vegetables at dawn. Sizzling pan-fried dumplings, dough flake soup in a pot wrapped in burlap, red-bean porridge and *kake udon* in small pots steaming over a fire, hulled-millet cakes, fried glass noodles, soft pork head meat, broiled sardines . . . I ate almost everything my stomach wanted and my tongue demanded. Greed was never-ending, and madness took hold of me. There was no way to put an end to it. Even good sense went away. I walked around feeling dizzy, as if I had a fever, and if I came across something I could put in my mouth, I did.

Finally, my stomach rejected the food. Then my tongue pushed it away. My stomach felt like it would explode. I thought something might spill out of me if I leaned slightly to one side. I finally left the market, waddling slowly. A heavy satiety weighed me down. But it wasn't the bursting satisfaction that pushed me to despair. I still yearned for something, even though I couldn't take another sip of water or eat a single bean. The money constantly demanded to buy new food. This was an unquenchable thirst.

Stuffed to stupefaction, I tottered home, dragging fullness from one ankle and deep despair as heavy as an iron ball from the other. Sobs rose from within. I thought of Mother and Sister, waiting for me in our ludicrous box in this toy-like city. My heart felt as if it would break to pieces. I thought my luck had run out. Tragedy was probably waiting for me at the end. I had nothing other than the empty mess kit, my empty pocket, and my greedy starving soul demanding more.

Future Daughter-in-law

Mother got up. This seemed to presage change.

It was a very cold day. The water in the bowl by my bed was frozen solid. The morning sun seemed to rise slower because of the cold. Even the sunlight that stained the window pink looked chilly. I glanced at the frost covering the ceiling and the walls. It was more delicate and cleaner than snow. It was as if I were lying in a shiny crystal box.

Mother walked in the door, her wet hair covering her thin shoulders. She put a small mirror on top of the old-fashioned chest and started brushing her hair. She parted it neatly, wound her hair into a bun, and slid a long hairpin through it. Her movements were peaceful, so quiet that she didn't seem to be moving at all.

Mother's health was worse than ever. Her face, usually alert and calm, had a yellowish swelling. Dark shadows deepened under her eyes, her nose and lips were bluish, and her thin neck and shoulders had a certain coldness to them, making me shiver. Worm-like veins were visible on her hands. I could see through her hands, as if they were transparent tropical fish. She was so thin that you couldn't feel her mass. She was like a paper doll; small,

light, and skinny. Seeing that Mother could still move about comforted me.

After doing her hair, Mother opened the chest. I thought she was
looking for her good clothes. I remembered going to Uncle's house.
Even though it had been a profitable trip, it remained a sad memory. I
didn't think she would go see him again. *Where was she going?*

Mr. Choe's appearance answered my question. She had suddenly
wanted to visit Father. Mother followed Mr. Choe out. It was her
first outing in a long time. A few women stood outside, looking at
her with sad expressions. Mother floated out of the alley, as if she
weren't moving at all.

They returned near sunset. Without saying a word to each other,
Mr. Choe went into the A-bomb patient Mr. Kim's house and Mother
came into ours. They both looked exhausted and cold. But Mother
didn't take to her bed. She remained crouched in front of the chest
for a long time with her head bowed, like a statue. Unable to hear
her breathing, I got scared, thinking she had passed away. I looked at
Sister, who didn't look up. For some reason, her cheeks were red.

Mother opened the chest and took out several outfits. They
weren't hers; they were all Sister's. And all of Sister—a look she
would give me, her smile, even her soft breath—lived in those outfits.
Everything I associated with her was interlaced with each thread.

Mother's eyes were damp when she turned toward us. It was
hard to see her tears because of the dark circles under her eyes. She
was obviously hiding a never-ending spring in her depths.

"Let's go, dear," Mother said to Sister in a voice I had never heard
before. "Father won't be coming home for a full year."

That was all she said.

Mother stood up, holding Sister's clothes. Sister was still blushing.

The alley was completely empty, probably because it was so cold. There wasn't a brat to be seen. Only the wind raked the alley, which was frozen like a long, narrow sewer.

Mother left the house and Sister followed. They looked like they were going somewhere far. Mother, clutching Sister's clothes to her chest, didn't look back once. But Sister turned around again and again, smiling at me. *Sister* . . . But I couldn't smile back. I felt like throwing stones at her. They turned a corner and vanished from my sight. The empty alley seemed as desolate as an open field. I looked down at my feet. *Now they will make a left to get to the house of Tofu Flesh, her four brothers, and mounds of tofu. That will be Sister's home from now on. She will be their future daughter-in-law.* The more I thought about it, the more incensed I became. I wanted to cry.

A Corpse Is Always a Stranger

One can't be a friend with a corpse because it is always a stranger. This is still true even if it's the corpse of a family member or neighbor. I can never imagine a corpse that looks like it's sleeping. Sleep exists in this world. Perhaps even death is something of this world. But a corpse doesn't belong here. It's something left behind by those who have departed this world. So a dead man's face is unfamiliar and awe-inspiring. Any memory about him is useless. Nothing that belongs to this world is willing to accept a dead man's body. His is such a cold, unfamiliar face, something people never saw in his lifetime. We can only shovel some dirt on his face.

Dead bodies were often found in the park. I had seen them the previous fall from time to time, in the park that once housed more refugees than the number of city residents. The bald hill and small trees testified to its past. My first encounter with a body was that of a man with a long neck. I couldn't figure out his age because a painful expression was frozen on his face. Small, thin, and barefoot, he was wearing an out-of-season shirt. There wasn't much else interesting about him. He was one of those people you could frequently see in the park, the ones who had left their hometowns. He looked as if he had carried his weight with his long neck.

Of course, I didn't know if there was another world other than this one. If there were such a place, the bridge that helped him go to the other world was a small tree. In the maple family, it was at the top of the bald hill, so you could see the entire city if you hung from the tree like that man. I knew this because I had spent almost a day in that tree. You could see everything; the city, the two railroad tracks going around the city, and beyond that, the toy-like shantytown. His body was found hanging there, but he was already gone. The only thing left behind was that unfamiliar corpse. *What was his last memory?* Nobody knew what he saw, or wanted to see, in his last moment on earth. At least one thing was clear. He probably hadn't wanted to see the things I could see myself, because he didn't have to hang himself there just to take in the destitute city and its neighborhoods.

I'd also come across neglected bodies. Neglected by their owners, by society, and finally by this world, they would rot so quickly. A good example was one man who had died after drinking a bottle of *soju* spiked with some kind of poison. I didn't feel awe. Flies, wind, and sunlight lingered on his body. There was no reason to throw dirt on him, since he was already on his way to disintegration.

Winter and ice came to the park. Corpses were found everywhere, left behind by the cold. The winter weather in the basin was temperamental and cruel. The city, unfortunately trapped in a raised valley, produced several people who froze to death each night. Their bodies were frequently found around the park, on the stone steps, in the dry sewer circling it, in the two shrines, and even under the stone engraved with a poem. They were stiffer than rocks and bleaker than the frozen, naked land.

What is winter cold? It's invisible. We can see only the scars it leaves behind. The corpses could be considered mere scars, too. But I thought I could see the true face of cold whenever I stood in front of the bodies. Its face was very similar to a single diminutive tree planted somewhere in the underworld, or to a *soju* bottle mixed with an unspecified poison.

—

I came across a woman's body lying near the middle of the stone steps. Hers was a small, pitiful corpse, looking as if it had been in the same spot for a long time. I stopped in front of it. I was alone. It was eerily cold without a ray of sunlight, even though it was midday. Hardly anyone was in the park. The body didn't stop the few people who climbed up the steps.

A sharp wind sliced through the empty park. But I was fine. Sometimes, combating the cold helped me forget my hunger. I looked down at the corpse. Her face was unfamiliar to me. I carefully looked over her narrow forehead pushed against the stone step, her thick hair cushioning her face, and her half-open, stiff, dry lips. Her two hands, which must have been busy until yesterday, were motionless between her chest and chin. Nobody would be able to get those thin and dirty hands to move again—they were in eternal rest. There wasn't any evidence pointing to struggle. She must have warmed up to the cold, to death, and to the loneliness of her last living moment. Her neat posture gave off the impression that the stone stairs propping her up were warm. She'd left nothing behind. Even her dead body wasn't hers. She parted with this world so completely and perfectly that her corpse, left behind on the stairs like a small, coiled pad, looked like a completely unfamiliar object.

I straightened up and looked around slowly. I spotted something I recognized. It was definitely hers—a bucket with a couple of rotten apples inside. I didn't need to revisit my memories from the previous fall. I looked back at the corpse again. I vaguely recognized that woman's face from the unfamiliar body. Her face had faded like an old memory. Perhaps it wasn't her face, but my memory of her I was seeing right then.

A man who looked like a park caretaker walked toward me, expressionless. But then he would have had no reason to be surprised. He probably had seen her every day last fall. He covered her neglected body with a sack he was carrying under his arm. The dead woman was curled into such a small ball that one sack was enough to cover her. The space she'd occupied in this world probably was not much bigger. Everything, from her hair to her toes, was concealed.

I walked down the steps slowly. The sky was still gray and frozen, without the slightest hint of sunlight. A gust of stinging wind knifed me in the chest. Suddenly the return trip seemed far. Shivering, I thought hard. My head throbbed. Amid all the memories and fantasies, the image of a few rotten apples was the only thing left at the end. Finally, I realized something. I recalled, as clearly as if a cold wind were sweeping through my head, that she had always eaten rotten apples. She would dig out the rotten parts with her dirty finger and eat them. She didn't eat anything else, the way Mother didn't take anything in except for water. I felt as if I would throw up.

Leaving behind her small, sad body, she had gone to the other world. She would never again come back to that decrepit park. I pictured the bucket and apples. She would obviously never eat or sell the rotten fruit. I felt sick.

That night, the A-bomb patient Mr. Kim died. Everyone was saddened by his death. It was as if we suddenly realized his misfortune, concealed till now thanks to his loyal brother. The man, who used to cross the borders of three or four countries as if hopping over woven fences, had spent almost ten years confined in that small room. What was it that Mr. Kim waited for? He had been waiting for death, spreading slowly from his feet toward his heart.

Mr. Choe bought a coffin and Mr. Gwak hung mourning lamps. The alley, which had been filled only with fierce cold wind since winter began, suddenly became crowded with well-wishers. Women wept as they peeked into the Kims' room. But Mrs. Kim didn't cry. She commanded her husband's funeral cheerfully, as if she had steeled herself for this day for the past ten years.

Mr. Kim, who had occupied a box-sized room while he was alive, took up even less space in death. His coffin was the smallest space I had ever seen. It was so tiny that there wasn't room for anything else other than his body. His wife and children hovered helplessly outside. There wasn't space for even his best friends, Mr. Choe and Mr. Gwak, to squeeze in. That was probably why they looked lonelier and sadder than usual.

For a long time, I looked out at the mourning lamps hanging at the end of the alley. I could see their faint light from our window. Snowflakes fell under that light, which was as bright as the space Mr. Kim had occupied.

Reverend Cha

O ne day, I went to church with Mother. The trek was very difficult and embarrassing. The roads were slippery and Mother couldn't walk without my help. I had never thought that the tented church on the hill was that far away. By the time we got there, struggling, I was completely drenched in cold sweat. I was cold and my legs trembled.

I didn't know why Mother decided to go to church all of a sudden. Their powdered milk supply had been depleted for a while. For some time, I had thought that the church could give us nothing more. The girl who'd had the seizure had told me that you could forget your hunger by praying, but that didn't work for me. So I couldn't understand why Mother had decided to attend church, this late.

Familiar faces hovered in the churchyard carpeted with coal dust. Some time ago, I had been a loyal participant as well. I felt embarrassed when I saw those familiar faces, but not just because of Mother. Thankfully, they didn't scold me, but greeted us warmly instead. They joyfully grasped our hands, as if they had found a lost mother and baby sheep. Their hands were frozen, but their grip warmed our hearts.

"Son, you've done a great job. Bless you," Reverend Cha, standing near the entrance, told me, patting my head. He was dressed up in a suit, though it was old, and was even wearing a tie.

—

I had heard some rumors about him. It was hard to tell whether he had a good or bad reputation among the shantytown residents. Someone said that he had seen Reverend Cha drunk. According to the witness, he had woven through the streets, his face red and drunk. Another piece of gossip was that some congregants had caught the Reverend watching a very suspicious movie in a third-rate theater on the outskirts of the city. Also, there was word that he had once fought with gangsters, and that creditors often hounded him. But of all of these rumors, the one that bothered everyone the most was the one about the "red bills." Apparently Reverend Cha never forgot to refer to "red bills" during his sermons, as if he were scolding the congregation. "Please don't take out red bills in front of God. It's embarrassing to offer snot-smeared one-won bills to God!" Since he never came to the children's classes, I had never heard this speech myself.

Of course, the stories behind the scenes explained each rumor. These made Reverend Cha respectable. For example, the drunken incident: According to someone, it was indeed true that Reverend Cha had been drunk. But it wasn't because he was abusing alcohol like the many drunkards in our neighborhood. He had drunk not liquor, but the residue obtained after straining that evil beverage. I understood all too well that the residue could not be considered evil, but necessary daily bread for us when mixed with a little saccharin.

So the criticism should have been directed not at Reverend Cha, who was visiting a congregant's house, but at the poverty of the latter. He hadn't had anything else to offer the Reverend. Even though the drunken incident was poverty's fault, it wasn't something that deserved criticism. I could imagine Reverend Cha sharing the food and offering prayer. The leftover alcohol in it would have made his untrained body sway.

The incident at the cinema proved to be similarly innocent. They say that the Reverend wasn't trying to see a scantily clad actress or a violent battle scene. He was studying the recent war, whose footage was inserted throughout the film. Apparently he stared at the masses of refugees coming down south, so transfixed that he couldn't even breathe.

Reverent Cha didn't have family, wealth, or belongings to speak of. He lived in one part of the tented church that was blocked off with a thick plank of wood and took his meals wherever there was food. During the day, he would go anywhere his feet took him. Despite all those rumors, nobody believed that he would keep even a mustard seed for himself. Reverend Cha was that kind of person. So the stories of fights with gangsters, of creditors hounding him, or of his going on about "red bills" during his sermons weren't ever counted against him. I, for one, believed that he had a bigger and nobler objective.

I felt very good, feeling Reverend Cha's hand on my head. I decided I would come to church every Sunday, even if they didn't give out powdered milk.

The wooden floor was so icy that our chins trembled. But Mother sat through a service from the very beginning to the end. She didn't know a single hymn or even one phrase of the Apostles' Creed. She knew only that prayers started with closed eyes and ended with "Amen." Since she made it to the church with difficulty after such a long illness, I was surprised that she was able to sit through the long, boring service. She didn't even look like she was in pain. She seemed more comfortable than she had looked lying on the warmest part of our small room.

The next day, Reverend Cha paid us a visit. I still remember the conversation he had with Mother after a prayer.

"Reverend, will my boy's father and sister be able to come home if I believe in Jesus?" This was her last wish.

I clearly heard Reverend Cha's easy answer. "Yes. Just pray to Jesus. Then the day will come when the entire family can live together."

Mother asked again, cautiously, "How does one pray, Reverend?"

Reverend Cha replied breezily, "Do it like you would to the Wise Old Goddess of Maternity."

As he left, he said he would try to get Mother to receive treatment, since it looked like her illness had become more serious. He never did talk about the miracles of Jesus that my Sunday school teachers would tell us. How much happier Mother would have been if he had told her about Jesus curing lepers, a paralyzed man, a mute, and saving a child possessed by evil spirits! I was disappointed, but didn't have the courage to ask him to mention these miracles. Reverend Cha left behind a few scoops of pressed barley he had brought in a paper bag and a small amount of money.

Noodles without Broth

S ister came to visit for the first time since she had gone to live at Tofu Flesh's.

"It's her brother's birthday so we're not working today," she said. But she didn't say which of Tofu Flesh's brothers' birthday it was. I didn't ask because I was still mad at her. Who cared whose birthday it was? I just hoped that it wasn't the legless brother.

Sister looked livelier than when she had been living at home. It was only natural, since she had been able to escape from poverty by leaving us. This fact made me madder. Her face would become plump and her skin white and soft, just like her friend Tofu Flesh. But she wouldn't be able to go meet boys, because she was the future daughter-in-law. She would have to be chaste, not wild like the daughter.

Sister gave us a few presents and produced a couple of carefully folded bills from her clothes. She seemed rather proud. "Mom, is there something you would like to eat?"

I quickly glanced at Mother. Sitting against the plank wall, she was contemplating something. I swallowed. I could gather what she was thinking.

—

A big change had come over Mother since we had started going to church. The best part was that she was regaining hope. Her wish was that our family could live together again. Mother obviously believed Reverend Cha's thoughts on this issue. After that first day, Mother had often gone back to church, and she would frequently sit at home facing the wall. She didn't say anything out loud, but I knew what she was doing. She was praying as sincerely as she would to the Wise Old Goddess of Maternity. Mother also began to eat, little by little. I thought it was a natural evolution. You might be able to live on God's words, but you couldn't do it only on water. But Mother had subsisted this long with only water. She couldn't sate her newfound appetite, but she also couldn't digest what she did eat. I pitied her. Pity!

Mother's transformation was hard for me to take. How could my small hands satisfy her appetite, which had become as demanding as a growing child's? The money she received for sending Sister away—putting it this way would have tormented her forever—was long gone. Winter wasn't over yet, but I was about to have to take the mess kit to the frozen streets again.

It pained Mother to be unable to digest the food she finally began to eat. A few times, Mother made mistakes, as a retarded kid would. It wasn't just because of her stomach, which had weakened by digesting only water for a long time. It didn't help that there were only three toilets in our neighborhood. It wasn't easy for Mother to go all the way there. After making a couple of mistakes, she finally did her urgent business in the room.

—

My expectations weren't for naught. After thinking for a long time, Mother opened her mouth. "What is it called? The Chinese noodles without broth." She was as embarrassed as a shy girl. I remembered the black-bean noodles that Mrs. Kim had given us once. It was the first and only day she had seen a doctor. "You mean black-bean noodles, right, Mom?" I said loudly, and she nodded with a smile.

Two bowls of noodles without broth were delivered. Sister declined to eat, so Mother and I had one each. We ate without stopping to breathe. The food we ate that day deserves to be called something fancier than "black-bean noodles" or "noodles without broth." But Mother christened it "noodles without broth." And that bowl of broth-less noodles was the last, best meal she had in this world.

Mother passed away before the sun set. An hour later, Mrs. Kim brought the doctor over. *She's miscarried.* Our belief—that she had died from severe indigestion—was incorrect. Taking his bag and getting up right away, the doctor said, "The fetus wasn't able to hang on because the mother was so weak. If you send someone later I'll write up a death certificate." I looked at him blankly. The man in the white coat still had delicate, soft skin like a woman. Mrs. Kim saw him to the door.

Even now, my throat closes in if I recall how pained Sister's sobs were. Our neighbors quickly filled the doorway to our room, but Sister, completely unself-conscious, writhed on top of Mother's body. Her death hadn't sunk in for me. I couldn't understand where such wretched, hot, and violent sobs could have been hidden in Sister's small body. From her bare feet to her disheveled hair, there wasn't a single part of her that wasn't crying hard. She fainted several times and writhed again upon waking. If Mrs. Kim hadn't finally slapped her and pulled her outside, we might have had another small corpse on our hands.

I Know How to Cry
Like a Mute

Mother's funeral was over the next day. It was a lonely funeral, without even a single mourning lamp. We couldn't have done anything without Mr. Choe's help. He stayed with us from right after Mother's death to the next day's cremation. Though a poor funeral, at least a bit of money would have been necessary. I don't know where we got the money—probably from the pockets of Mrs. Choe, Mrs. Kim, and Mr. Gwak. Perhaps even Tofu Flesh's family had pitched in as well. I remember that Mr. Choe even gave me some money after the funeral. Though poor, their hearts were undoubtedly generous.

We said goodbye to Mother at the river, which we had crossed perilously to gather fallen fruit the previous summer. It wasn't easy, as the river was frozen solid. We had to walk on the ice to get to the middle of the river. I got scared because Mr. Choe kept warning us to be careful from behind me. But Sister, having gotten over her violent sorrow, was numb to everything. The water in the middle of the river looked colder and clearer because of the ice. It was a sunny day, although the wind was frigid. The light danced brilliantly on the surface of the water. So when we slowly scattered Mother, transformed into a fistful of dust, into the river, I was blinded by the brightness. I briefly envisioned a swarm of dragonflies flying up, brilliant and transparent.

We had noodle soup for lunch on our cold and lonely way home. We hadn't eaten anything for an entire day. Mr. Choe and I each emptied a pot with gusto, but Sister only sipped the broth once or twice. I felt bad. I was worried that Sister would end up in bed like Mother, but I didn't reveal my thoughts.

The alleys in our neighborhood were empty. I noticed that emptiness more than at any other time. The ground coated with the messy coal dust, the sewer, frozen over along with trash, the roofs thatched with pieces of cans, and the shoddy plank walls—their colors couldn't have been more vivid. The dummy school at the end of the alley was quiet too. Only a dusty swing swayed in the schoolyard. Winter vacation probably wasn't over yet. *What are the mutes doing now?* I wondered. For some reason, I couldn't stay calm any longer.

If in the alley we hadn't bumped into the girl who'd had the seizure, I wouldn't have been able to suppress my emotions. She was with her father. Though leaning on a cane because of his injured back, he was walking without his daughter's help. It was a very labored walk. She smiled brightly, "My father can walk by himself!"

Mother's death finally sank in when we returned to our small room. The warmest part of the room where Mother and her water bowl had lain for so long was the first thing that caught my eye. Nothing was there, neither Mother nor her water bowl. Suddenly, I felt a sharp pain in my heart, as if I had been shot with an arrow. I couldn't express Mother's absence with words. I squatted with my back against the wall. I couldn't stop the sobs from erupting. I buried my face into my knees, hugging them. But I didn't shed any tears. I had finally learned to cry like a mute.

part 3

Judas's Hour

The Hunt

W e went hunting every night. Last fall's activity of choice—
capturing dragonflies—was nothing compared to this.
We never got excited about that anymore. The empty fall, bare winter, and hungry spring were gone. Summer teemed with evil, and
we were completely preoccupied with the nightly hunts that started
around then.

We met every evening at the railroad tracks near our neighborhood. When the sun lumbered behind the red hill in the park, darkness would slowly blanket our toy-like neighborhood. The camouflage army tents and the tarpaulin roofs would gently fade into the
dark, and that was when we would all gather at the railroad tracks.

Before each hunt, one of the older boys would conduct roll
call. So grown-up that he would have been sent to war had it gone
on a year longer, the boy never forgot to do this. We were almost
always all there unless something unexpected happened. Nobody
was forced to come. The joy of hunting had captured us so completely that none of us could ignore this exciting game. Of course,
there would be the rare times when someone failed to come. Our
departure would be delayed on those days, and the absent kid

would be condemned. Everyone would look around in the dark
and grumble.

"Which son of a bitch is it? Asshole . . ."

"Isn't it that Seoul kid Tae-gil? I don't see him, do you?"

"Yeah, that asshole didn't come again. We have to kick him out!"

Eight or nine out of ten times, it was Tae-gil who was missing.
But I understood his situation. As we all knew, he had an eccentric
single mother who beat him every day. It was an inevitable tragedy
that couldn't come to an end unless his mother changed her belief that
whipping her son was the only way to protect him from the rough and
dark times. So whenever his beatings, his daily bread, were too severe,
poor Tae-gil would miss the hunt. His strange mother's blind belief
wasn't solely to blame. No matter how harsh and severe the beating,
it couldn't ward off the world's evil. Then again, most of the other
parents thought the same thing, too. So I could only hope that everyone would sympathize with poor Tae-gil's misfortune. But the kids
would continue to complain and curse at him for a while longer.

Our hunting grounds were the dark streets of the city. The streets,
still marred by the remains of the war, were rough and desolate even
during summer nights. Because of the limited supply of power, street-
lights were rarely on. The darkness fanned our adventurous spirit.
Many blind spots existed in the quiet streets; they set the stage for
our hunts. We advanced as stealthily as an invading army and quickly
deployed toward a single trap in the dark. The hunt was about to start.
Each time, feeling the hot summer night air suddenly touch my skin
and wrap around me like a cold wet cloth, I would shiver violently.

Bait was required to lure our victim. The older boys always chose
carefully. We needed one on which anyone could nibble, so usually

the smallest or the weakest-looking one was picked. He would be the main player in the hunt. It was the most exhilarating role, and I was lucky to have been chosen several times. How could anyone fully imagine the thrill? I paraded around like an emperor. I was afraid of no one. With one hand stuck jauntily under my belt and the other gripped into a tight fist, I would whistle "The Number Twelve Train to Seoul" and "Silla's Moon-lit Night" through my teeth.

Of course, my cockiness was only possible because the other kids were hiding in the darkness behind me. But, amazingly, I always forgot that. Even though I was small and weak, I believed that I had an amazing strength hidden inside me. My arms and legs felt strong and my heart was on fire. I picked fights with everyone, swore like a sailor, and swung my small fists fearlessly. I may have been better than anyone else in luring people into our trap, as I was usually praised effusively afterward.

Our hunts were always successful. Everyone was easily caught in our trap. Nobody who fearlessly bit our bait came out of it unharmed. We didn't care who our victim was, and it didn't matter even if he realized his rashness quickly. We popped out of the darkness even before he let go of the bait, swarmed around him like bees, and poured intense fire onto him. Nobody could fight us off. It was usually over in a minute or two. Even those who fought back at first would soon be subdued and fall to their knees. But I don't think it was only because there were so many of us. If it were simply a victory of numbers, I don't think hunting could have captivated us as it did. I still remember the crazed way we pecked at our prey and the deep, sweet sleep I would drop into at home afterward.

Gang's Barbershop

I t wasn't just we kids who were engrossed in hunting games. The adult world was also engaged in similar activities. The incidents involving Gang's Barbershop were a good example.

There were at least five or six barbershops in our shantytown, but only one had a sign on its door. The rest were unlicensed. Many differences existed between the two kinds, from the facilities and the skills of the employees to the price and the types of customers. It's foolish to think twice as to which establishment we kids frequented. We were satisfied with our shaved, prickly, chestnut burr-like heads revealing dry patches, and didn't care about facilities or skills or service. Sometimes we would even squat in the streets and entrust our heads to an itinerant barber.

The unlicensed barbershops didn't have any chairs to speak of. The makeshift chairs, made of rough planks, seemed to have been made with the barber's comfort in mind, not that of the customer. Plus, the clippers with missing teeth and the barber's bumbling skills and lack of care guaranteed that your hair would look chewed up. My heart would drop when the barber picked up the razor. Getting a haircut was an immense ordeal. Sometimes you would even get ringworm from the contaminated clippers.

If you took all of this into consideration, the sole legal barbershop in the neighborhood might as well have been on another planet. It had three metal chairs, most definitely built for the customer's comfort, several skilled barbers, and a white-coated female beautician. They would wash your hair with warm water all year round, take care of your face, clip your fingernails and toenails, and trim the hair growing from your ears and nose. Not everyone living in the shantytown was poor, so the barbershop thrived. Among the people I knew, Mr. Gwak, Mr. Choe, Tofu Flesh's father and four brothers, the owner of the velour factory, and the owner of the radio repair shop were all regulars. Also, Mr. Kim the A-bomb patient would, when he was alive, call a barber and beautician to his home and get his hair cut, and Tough Widow's son-in-law, despite living off her, would go to the barber more frequently than anyone else. Anyway, if you were one of them, you were among the chosen of our shantytown. The majority of the residents, including my friends and me, could only look at them with envy.

But that barbershop had a major flaw. "Kang's Barbershop" was carved clearly on the sign in relief, but we usually referred to it as Gang's Barbershop. The owner was a young man named Kang. He was the youngest of three barbers, and had a slim waist and clear skin like a woman. He was always neat and stylish. His collar was impeccably clean and his head, styled with plenty of pomade, never had a single hair out of place. Sometimes when he had nothing to do, he would swivel one of the chairs toward the window and look quietly into the sunny street. His gaze was as cold and peaceful as his appearance. If we were peeking in the barbershop and were caught by that gaze, we would quickly shy away. We wouldn't be able to move our legs. It was because he was such a mystery to us.

His fairly busy barbershop also saw a lot of unwelcome guests, men who depended on their fists and guts to survive in the shantytown and the marketplace. They would come into the barbershop whenever they wanted to kill time or create a scene. During slow afternoons, they would shave, wash their faces, make dirty jokes, and take over empty chairs and snore, while the employees glared at them. We started calling it Gang's Barbershop partly because of those men. Timid customers would be startled and turn around at the door. The biggest liability of the barbershop was that it seemed to be a gangsters' meeting place. Normally the management might have done something about this situation, but nobody made that kind of effort there. Mr. Kang didn't seem to mind the unwelcome guests or their rude behavior. Of course, fists, rather than law, ruled our world. Still, we didn't think Mr. Kang left them alone because he was unconfident with his fists.

He was, as I've said before, a mysterious person. He looked as frail as a girl and seemed to be the kind of effeminate man that lives off a *gisaeng*, but he possessed a murderous strength and a blade-like coldness concealed inside. He was known to have been a member of some kind of special unit in the war, and he apparently had crossed the threshold of death day and night. People said that those he killed could have formed a sizeable platoon, and that the weight of the medals he received for distinguished war services added up to one *gwan* in weight. We never heard any tales of adventure from him. And we had never seen even one of his many medals. I think even the people who gossiped about his heroics hadn't ever seen them either. But we believed those stories, as Mr. Kang would reveal his immense abilities once in a while, as if to build on our belief in him.

The first frightening incident happened the previous spring. Kang's Barbershop had been open for less than a month. A man, thrown through the big glass door of the barbershop, rolled out onto the street. We had been snooping around there at the time, and we leapt back, frightened. He was bald and aging. We thought he would never stand again. But he jumped up and assumed a defensive stance. We couldn't close our mouths. We realized that he wasn't an ordinary man. Blood trickled down his forehead like thin snakes. His eyebrows scrunched together, he glared murderously at the doorway.

"Asshole, you better come out here!" he shouted. "I'm not dead yet, fucker! You asshole!" His confident shouts were hollow, however. Mr. Kang appeared from the wrecked doorway. He was as neat as usual. His collar was impeccable and his pomaded hair was still in place. Only his eyes were glistening, colder than ever before.

Our shock was great. We didn't yet know anything about Mr. Kang. He was only the girlish-looking young owner of the new barbershop. But the opponent was, though old, someone who seemed like a seasoned hand in the underworld. Even at the last moment, we couldn't imagine that Mr. Kang would be able to stand up to him.

It was over in an instant. Our expectations were completely overturned. It was such a shock that it captured our hearts. For days afterward, the incident was the only thing we talked about. We couldn't forget it, as if we had witnessed a stirring scene from a movie. We saw Mr. Kang's icy cold glare, his slim woman-like waist bending midair like a bow, and the ends of his four limbs flying forward and targeting the opponent's weak spots sharply and precisely. The man's resistance was pitiful. Falling powerlessly, he couldn't get up again.

But this was only the prologue. After that day, similar scenes often played out at Kang's Barbershop. The main actor was usually Mr. Kang, who always won. The opponents changed each time but nobody ever beat him. Sometimes a weapon appeared like a prop, and other times a group of people participated, but the results were always the same. It was thanks to Mr. Kang's heroic moves, and also because his thuggish guests would help him out whenever necessary.

Anyway, despite his frail appearance, the mysterious Mr. Kang looked more and more like a giant, and Gang's Barbershop seemed like his kingdom. We were soon wishing for a strong opponent who would be a better match. Of course, we wondered why they acted out such dramatic scenes. But we weren't interested in the possible answers, only in the bloody fights. We didn't care to give it deep thought. Instead, we came to a quick conclusion—that those men liked to play those games, similar to the way we loved to hunt at night.

The Queen Ant and Soldier Ants

A shocking incident happened at Gang's Barbershop at the peak of our nightly hunts. Mr. Kang, who had never before experienced failure, suffered a temporary defeat.

It had rained on and off at the end of a series of blazing hot days. It looked like we were on the verge of the rainy season, since the sky had been overcast from morning. We were fidgety, having been cooped up inside all day. Because it was wet outside, we probably wouldn't hunt that night. After eating dinner at the tofu factory—more accurately getting handouts—and coming home unhappy, I bumped into Tae-gil.

"It happened! Something's happened!" he said, out of breath.

"Where?"

"What do you mean where, of course it's at Gang's Barbershop. But Mr. Kang lost completely!"

I felt a sudden shock, as if I had been electrocuted. I didn't waste time looking at Tae-gil's breathless face. We started sprinting toward the barbershop.

The drama was already over. With all the major players gone, only the empty stage awaited me. But I wasn't disappointed, because even that scene overwhelmed me. The shop was almost completely empty. The appliances and instruments were in their places, but there weren't any employees or the owner, not to mention customers. Only the female beautician was standing near the entrance. I had never seen such a frightened woman. She was mumbling something in a trembling voice to the people who had gathered, but nobody seemed to understand what she was saying.

"The guy with one arm stabbed Mr. Kang with the hook on his fake arm," whispered Tae-gil, still breathless. "Look, there's the blood!"

I shuddered. I had finally noticed the spilled blood on the ground, spreading from the doorway to the alley. Because of the darkening day, it looked like a bucket of black ink had been dumped there.

They said that Mr. Kang was taken to the hospital on the back of another barber. Now that a powerful opponent had appeared, I felt torn for a split second. We had always wished for a stronger opponent, but it wasn't because we felt some kind of animosity toward Mr. Kang. We had no reason to dislike him. He was our hero, our idol. We never wished for his destruction, but continued to believe in and worship him. But now it was as if we had been hoping for his downfall.

Tae-gil chattered on the way home. "Even though Mr. Kang lost, the asshole wasn't fighting fair. I heard he stabbed him from behind."

I didn't reply. I was depressed and upset. Tae-gil kept going on angrily, insisting that this match didn't count because the opponent hadn't fought fair.

"They have to fight again. We'll find out who really is stronger only if they do it officially. But I don't know if Mr. Kang will live. I saw people carrying him out, and his head was banged up."

Even after such a big incident, Gang's Barbershop was open for business the next day. We took it as a good sign that Mr. Kang wasn't hurt badly. But when we saw that one-armed man in the barbershop, we were disgusted, as if we had accidentally bit on a bug hiding in our food. How could we have even imagined it? The one-armed man came back the next day, and even sat on an empty chair turned toward the window like Mr. Kang used to, and looked out calmly into the fine rain. We felt sick when we saw him. We became angrier because he poked at the window ledge with his metal hook, with which he'd smashed Mr. Kang's head.

"Coward!"

"Does he think he's the owner? Motherfucker!"

We were enraged more than was necessary, as if we were the ones who had been robbed of the barbershop. We spat, cursed, and gave him the finger endlessly. Of course, all of this happened out of his line of vision.

He really acted as if he were the owner. According to rumors, he meddled with the way things were run in the shop. The employees always looked annoyed because he kept interfering, saying that they were unfriendly, the service wasn't good, and the atmosphere wasn't nice. We could only imagine how they felt, since we, uninvolved in the whole thing, were so angry.

Fortunately we didn't have to endure his presence for more than ten days. One afternoon, when the sky was clearing up after a long period of thick clouds and intermittent rain, we walked by Kang's Barbershop and saw Mr. Kang inside. We froze in our places, speechless.

Mr. Kang hadn't changed much. He looked a bit pale and his head was bandaged, but he was still dressed neatly. As in the old days, he was sitting on his chair and looking out quietly at the summer sun pouring onto the alley, which looked as if coarse grains of sand were being tossed down from above. His gaze was, as usual, cold and peaceful. The one-armed man was nowhere to be seen. The employees went about their business silently. They were calm, instead of looking annoyed as they had been for the past few days. The beautician was concentrating on cleaning out the ears of a regular. It was hard to believe, but the one-armed man with the metal hook in his sleeve was gone.

Nobody knew how Mr. Kang reclaimed his kingdom from the cowardly man. The one-armed man never appeared again. Thanks to this incident, the residents had something to gossip about for a long time. According to rumors, Mr. Kang wasn't actually the owner of the barbershop. The more interesting tidbit was that the owner was a woman, a widow with significant wealth, abilities, and beauty. Some said she was in her fifties, and others said she was only in her early thirties, and nobody knew which was true. She apparently ran two fairly big tearooms on the tearoom row at the heart of the city. Mr. Kang was a mere employee who enjoyed a special relationship with her.

I still remember how Mr. Gwak described their relationship. "So it's like the queen ant and a soldier ant. Of course, that's only if the rumors are true. There's only one queen ant but many soldier ants. The strongest one gets to serve the queen. Hey, Mr. Choe! Isn't that a funny world?" Then he laughed heartily.

Thirst

O ur nightly hunts were at their peak around this time. We went out almost every night and were always successful. But thirst accompanied our success. The more enthusiastic we were about the hunts and the more we succeeded, the thirstier we became. If our victim didn't resist at all and gave in weakly, we felt an intense anger toward him. We would direct even more violence at the coward on his knees pleading for mercy. But our thirst remained unquenched. On those days, we didn't feel like hunting and everything in the world seemed pointless. We would throw stones on our way home. Like splintered bombs, the stones carried the twisted desire and thirst still in our hearts into the night.

Sometimes we hunted girls. Once we hunted three, who had been wandering around without fear, at the same time. But we didn't beat them up. We only made lewd remarks and fondled them clumsily, while they whined unsuccessfully and shed troubled tears. The older boys, who watched from the sidelines, took them along when we let them go, and we went home feeling empty. I couldn't fall asleep easily on those nights.

Sometimes our thirst was quenched satisfactorily, like when we targeted Big Nose.

A cinema stood at the edge of a market near our neighborhood. It was a third-rate cinema on the outskirts of the city, in an old, renovated, Japanese occupation-era warehouse. The seats, hammered together from two long planks of wood so narrow you could barely fit your bottom on them, were all at the same height. During the summer, the inside smelled like mold and piss.

The cinema was always packed with people. Sometimes, if a Korean movie or a live show were playing, the cinema would be filled with people from our neighborhood and the market. From early morning, the familiar voice of the film interpreter called to the audience from the large speaker hanging from the roof of the cinema, and a clown, wearing a sandwich board sign, walked through the alleys of the neighborhood, ringing a bell like a tofu vendor.

We always ran to the cinema even though we didn't have any money. We stood in front, desperate to get in, and looked at the large pictures, the posters pasted everywhere, and the old still photographs.

— THE OPERETTA TROUPE LUXURY SHIP PERFORMS THE TRAGEDY "LEAVE, YEONG-JA." WRITTEN BY BAEK U-SAM. DIRECTED BY KIM HWA-RANG.

— HILARIOUS COMEDY SHOW "LUCKY WITH SONS AND DAUGHTERS," TWENTY SCENES IN TOTAL, SPECIAL GUEST APPEARANCE BY KIM JEONG-GU, HYEON IN, BAK DAN-MA, AND CANARY SHIN.

— THE WOMEN'S KOREAN MUSIC TROUPE SILLA PERFORMS THE CLASSICAL OPERA "BRIDEGROOM" (4 ACTS 6 SCENES) DIRECTED BY JO GEUM-AENG AND COMPANY.

If such programs were offered, the front of the cinema would be more crowded than the marketplace. The enormous crowd seemed to prove that all the nearby residents had come, except for the deaf, the blind, and the infants. We kids would push our way through the forest of people, hoping we could enter by luck. But this luck was hard to come by. We were often caught right at the last moment and chased out, getting a kick on our bottoms or a tap on the head. We were extremely mad when this happened. We would glare at the skinny man with eyes like those of a poisonous snake guarding the entrance like a bulldog. This was Big Nose. Apparently, he had been pretty well known as a boxer, even though it was in the country, and he had a broken nose as if to testify to his heyday. We hated him, but we'd turn away, unable to do anything about it.

But sometimes we were able to sneak in—I'm not sure how—so I can still remember the movies we saw around that time. Yi Min and Jo Mi-ryeong in "Tale of Chunhyang," Yi Hyang and Yun In-ja in "The Hand of Fate," Choe Eun-hee and Hwang Nam in "Dream," Marcel Carné's "Children of Paradise," Alan Ladd and Virginia Mayo in "The Iron Mistress" . . . These films moved me immensely and provided great fodder for my imagination.

I wanted to own a cinema. I wished that Sister, instead of working at the tofu factory, was a janitor at the cinema. I thought I could be happy if I were the kid selling popsicles and gum there. But I couldn't expect those things to happen any time soon, so I turned back sadly each time.

The third-rate cinema heightened our thirst. Even if our selection of Big Nose as our victim of the day could be seen as a random act, our animosity toward him was a subconscious factor. We were already tired of picking easy prey, which made the game boring and only made us thirstier. We wanted a stronger and more challenging prey, and Big Nose happened to cross our path around this time.

I was the day's bait. I sauntered haughtily around the trap. I let a weak-looking middle school student go, as well as a girl with short hair. I wanted to catch a brawny high school senior, or one of those guys who swaggered about because they play sports. I had finished "The Number Twelve Train to Seoul" and was whistling the last verse of "Silla's Moon-lit Night," when a tall man walking past me spat out, "Hey, what do you think you're doing, you little rat bastard?"

My lips froze instantly, but not because I was insulted. I had realized it was Big Nose. He rapped me lightly on the head and shuffled on. My whole body burned up. I looked behind me quickly and confirmed the presence of dozens of eyes shining in the darkness.

"Hey, Big Nose!" I yelled, without even realizing it.

His head whipped around. I started backing up, yelling clearly, "Eat shit, you fucker!"

I don't remember what exactly happened after that. He rushed toward me like a rabid dog, and I heard my friends running forward from the darkness behind me. Then we all became one big ball and rolled around for a while.

He was clearly a challenging opponent. As if proving his job or his past accomplishments, he resisted roughly and strongly, like a wild animal caught in a trap. But we were too many for him. Also, one of the older boys, panicking, used a sharp object he had sometimes brandished to intimidate victims but had never actually used, bringing Big Nose to his knees in defeat. Both sides were dealt huge blows. It was difficult to distinguish between the hunter and the hunted.

We slowly recovered after the intense fighting was over. We were shocked at our success. What an immense victory! We returned to the railroad tracks and lay around like a gaggle of defeated soldiers. We couldn't believe our victory. We still felt the pain from being kicked and pummeled. But we were victorious since our opponent had admitted defeat.

"That asshole Big Nose is just tall, not that strong," someone moaned in the darkness, and we became more animated. We all started putting in our two cents worth.

"Yeah, he's weaker than I thought. He's nothing, really."

"He got destroyed today. Did you guys see it? He couldn't do anything when he was stabbed right here, and then he hobbled away like a dog."

"Now he knows how strong we are. Should we go see a movie tomorrow?"

In spite of the chatter, we were all trembling violently in the darkness.

The Smell of a Rusted Gun

The rainy season arrived in the middle of summer that year, and everything became muddy. The shantytown was filled with water, and our small rooms and our just-as-small hearts were saturated with dampness. Everything was wet and smelled like mold. It was such an annoying, disgusting season.

I had experienced the rainy season in this valley the year before, soon after we moved to this city. But the previous year's wasn't as annoying. Granted, I couldn't sell red-bean buns with Sister, and Father's punch jar idled on top of the wooden cart, getting wet. Mother had felt bad that we had to eat cold buns three meals a day. And it was annoying to go to the refugee school beyond the park, whose yard turned into a muddy beach, wash my feet at the pump outside, file through the bullies' checkpoint, and sit in a swimming pool-like class. If you think about it, it's no surprise that the whole thing was such a bother.

But I couldn't remember feeling peeved. This year, alone in the empty room, I thought of still-absent Father, Mother who would never come back, and Sister who labored at Tofu Flesh's house as a future daughter-in-law. In my dreams, I would be transported back to last summer or spring. We would once again give up selling buns and Father would trade in the wooden cart for a secondhand bicycle. Mother would be crying quietly into her skirt on the moving truck, leaving our hometown behind. Sister would be smiling brightly and I would be whistling. When I woke up, the damn rain would still be pounding on the roof and the corners of my eyes would be wet.

I often skipped breakfast and lunch. I had no desire to go to the tofu factory in the rain just to fill my beggar's stomach. I didn't really want to see Sister, and I especially didn't want to see Tofu Flesh's brother, the one without a leg. I might have felt humiliated because he was my future brother-in-law, which Tae-gil liked to rub in my face whenever he was mad at me. In truth, I was more upset that, of Tofu Flesh's four brothers, Sister had chosen the guy who had left his leg behind at the battlefield.

Sister would come to see me if I didn't show up for dinner. She would spread out the food she had brought hidden in her skirt and quietly leave. She might have already noticed my sullenness toward her. She was always careful not to hurt my feelings. Sometimes, when she didn't have to work at night, she would come and sleep in our room.

But I was hostile toward her. She had definitely become healthier than last winter, gaining weight like Tofu Flesh. I had seen Sister smiling brightly inside the misty workroom. I had noticed that, despite the hard work and being treated contemptuously, she was happy. She, who had been so depressed when Father left and Mother died, had finally found bliss at Tofu Flesh's house, with the one-legged man. Her health and happiness made me dislike her even more. Sometimes I felt as if I hated her. It was when I smelled something unpleasant on her—the rusted gun smell I had once smelled on

Uncle, who had lost not a leg but an arm in the war. Tofu Flesh's leg-less brother had the same smell. One night, when Sister was asleep next to me, he came into our room. Nobody can blame him. Sister was his future wife and I was his future brother-in-law, whether I liked it or not.

We just stared at the confident intruder, who was completely wet. Rain soaked him outside and liquor paralyzed his soul. When he spread-eagled in the middle of the small room, I honestly wanted to hit him over the head with my bamboo pillow. But Sister behaved strangely. She had looked surprised but soon regained her composure. She peeled each layer of clothing off his body, which was sprawled across the floor like a rice sack, and dried off his hair, face, and body—things she couldn't strip off him—with a towel. Speechless, I just stared at her. *Sister is not normal*, I resisted. *She's crazy.* But she certainly didn't look crazy. Her face was expressionless, but quiet and collected. "Help me," she said in a low voice. I couldn't refuse even though I hated them both. We moved him to one side of the room with difficulty, and that's when I saw his fake leg. The leg was cold and strange even under the dim thirty-watt bulb. I remembered Uncle and his rusted gun smell suddenly, as if something sharp stabbed my heart.

I slept fitfully. I was digging. All sorts of weapons spilled out wherever I dug in our neighborhood. An M-1, a mortar shell, a broken sword, a part of a tank, a piece of aluminum with a number inscribed in it, a broken helmet . . . All of these things, with their varied sizes, shapes, and uses, were rusted over. Shocked, having never witnessed the war, I shouted, "It's here! This is where a battle took place . . ." I woke up.

It was getting bright outside. The one-legged man was in deep sleep, and Sister was sitting by me, dressed neatly. "Are you getting sick? You were talking in your sleep." She placed a hand on my forehead.

"Get off me!" I yelled, surprising myself, and pushed her hand away. I pulled my blanket over my head. I suddenly despised her. I could smell the rusted gun odor from her hands and body.

A Smaller Box

I visited Tae-gil's little room often. The rainy season continued, so we couldn't go hunting at night. I couldn't traipse through the muddy alleys like a puppy even though I was fidgety. Trapped inside a small box twenty-four hours a day, I just wanted to swear at everything. Tae-gil's room was a great place to get away from it all. That is, only if his eccentric mother was out.

Like many other shantytown residences, their house was a rectangular box. One side of the room was shut off with a few sheets of thin wood planks, and that was Tae-gil's room. Narrow and dark, it was a smaller box set within a slightly bigger box. Even though Tae-gil lived only with his mother, I never wondered why he had a room to himself, when everyone else with bigger families lived in one room. In any case, that room was a great place to play in.

The rain continued to come down. Sometimes, hail drummed on the roof. Even though everything was saturated with water, we were safe in the small ark. *Rain*, we yelled, giggling, *pour down, we'll give you steamed beans! Come on down, we'll give you boiled potatoes!* Then we flicked our middle fingers up to the sky and shouted in unison, "Your mother's cunt! Fuck your mother!"

A secret world was hiding in the smaller box inside the bigger one. That world was liberating, cozy, and filled with a kind of secretive mood. In that world, our destitute hearts were full and rich. Tae-gil was always cheerful in that room, as if he had never received a beating from his mother. We would look at each other and smile stupidly, make strange noises, and stand on our heads.

Tae-gil brought in all kinds of interesting random objects he had salvaged like a mouse from the nooks and crannies of his mother's room. But I won't list them all here. There were some things that are embarrassing to mention even now. I touched a condom for the first time in Tae-gil's room. Of course, we didn't really know what it was for. But I would be lying if I said that we didn't have the foggiest idea about its use. We looked at it with great curiosity, stuck our fingers inside and flipped it out, and even tried to blow it up like a balloon. "It's made in the U.S.," Tae-gil said, putting it back in its case.

There were many other things as well. The worn Korean playing cards, with which his mother checked her fortune every morning, mahjong and Korean chess pieces left behind by the old men who visited his house, chestnut-sized bean *yut*, an antique hourglass-shaped drum, American cigarettes, a not-yet-empty liquor bottle . . . These things captivated us. Time passed very quickly. It seemed as if time were being stolen from us in Tae-gil's room. So we had to hurry in order to do everything we wanted to in the limited time. We played with all the objects, and after that we smoked the American cigarettes, coughing and tearing up, and finally we even sipped the liquor. Even though we were clumsy, this was a fun game we could play only in that small world.

But our secretive games came to an end. It's foolish to expect that his mother wouldn't have noticed anything, even though Tae-gil was very good at covering our tracks. One day, she came home much earlier than expected, and we got caught. For a while, she glared coldly at the two small animals in a trap. It looked like she was wondering how to punish us to her satisfaction. We were cowed by the murderous look she was giving us. Looking at my feet, I thought that she would start by biting off our heads. Poor Tae-gil was stripped of his clothes. He was whipped severely and chased outside, naked from the waist down. Though he usually screamed when beaten, this time he was silent. He trembled like an abused dog in the rainy alley.

It was my turn, but she didn't strip or beat me. She dragged me to Sister instead. Grabbing my ear roughly, she paraded through the narrow alleys of the neighborhood, hollering that I was—to borrow her words—"this good for nothing that doesn't even deserve to drown in shit," who was a bad influence on her innocent son. Sister was intimidated. Tae-gil's mother shouted, "If his father is in the joint, at least his sister should keep an eye on him!" Sister blanched. Tofu Flesh's entire family ran out, as well as the neighbors. But for some reason I was unruffled.

That night, Sister came to our room. She didn't say anything but cried late into the night. Curled up like a shrimp next to me, she cried quietly for a long time. Her weeping was as long and tenacious as the rainy season. The last time she'd cried like that was when Mother died. I pretended I was asleep. There was little else I could do. Thankfully, she didn't smell like a rusted gun. Maybe her copious tears had washed away that unpleasant odor. I couldn't sleep, but felt comforted for once.

Thin, Weak Hands

*T*iring of itself, the long rainy season was on the verge of waning. Heavy clouds, which had pressed down on our neighborhood like sheets of dark rock beds, thinned, and bright sunlight burst forth several times a day.

Waking suddenly, I realized that someone was sitting by my side. It was dawn. *Father!* Something made me think that. The thought quickly shot through my dreamy consciousness like an arrow. I sat up to make sure. It was Father. I was dumbfounded. Father, who had gone out on his rattling secondhand bicycle, had returned home exactly a year later. I thought blankly of the things that had happened while he was gone. I couldn't remember anything. I recalled the frozen riverbed—where was it?—and vaguely remembered Sister walking down the alley with Mother, who clutched her daughter's clothes to her chest. Suddenly, the many nights of listening for the rattling bicycle flashed in my head. Sorrow, as dim as my memories, started to fill me up.

I opened the door and looked out. I didn't see the bicycle. Only the weak summer dawn light was shining down on the wet sawdust and coal powder strewn about in the alley. I hadn't forgotten my visit to the prison with Mr. Choe. Still, I couldn't understand Father's return. The way he crept back quietly—burglar-like, when everyone else was still sleeping, without his bicycle—seemed sudden and strange. Father remained silent for a long time—at least it seemed long to me. His head between his knees, he didn't move. I had never seen his hair that short. That might be another reason why I couldn't believe that Father was home. Two whorls and a huge scar, which must have been hidden all this time, were visible on his unfamiliar head.

"When was it?" Father's voice was muffled, as if it were coming from far away. He slowly raised his head and looked at me. His face was as familiar to me as my own small palm. I understood what he was asking, but I couldn't answer. I tried to remember the exact date, but it wasn't easy. Winter . . . last winter's cold, the riverbank frozen solid, a handful of gray powder, and the warm broth of the noodle soup we ate on the way home . . . Apart from these vague scenes, only the hard sorrow of that day flooded my heart. I felt a chill boring through my heart that early summer morning. Father didn't ask again. His hollow gaze swept across the empty room, where we had all slept squashed together. He looked at the space where Mother and Sister should have been. The tiny room must have seemed as endlessly wide as a barren field in winter to him.

"It was probably the second day of the last lunar month," Father said after a long while, dropping his head again. "I . . . sensed it. I had a nightmare and then a few days later I received Mr. Choe's urgent telegram, saying that your mother was very sick . . . Then that was it. I waited and waited but there wasn't any other news. When I thought about it later, your mother must have already been dead by then . . . It must have been the day of my bad dream and when Mr. Choe wrote me, which was the second day of the last lunar month."

He was barefoot. I saw a few tears drop onto his thin feet and seep into his skin. A sudden torrent of words burst out of me: "Sister lives at the tofu factory. It's her friend Tofu Flesh's house. They're very rich. She has four older brothers . . . Mother sent her. Sister didn't dislike the idea either. So she took all her clothes and things . . ." But I didn't reveal that she had gone there to work for free until she was old enough to become their daughter-in-law. I don't think it was just for Father's sake, but for mine as well. Naively, I thought Sister would have to come back home now that Father was back. "Sometimes she comes here and sleeps over. I eat at their house every day too . . ."

Father didn't say anything else. With his head still between his knees, he didn't look up or open his mouth again until morning came. Frozen, he looked like a small boulder. Closing my mouth, I looked at his big, thin hands. Those hands had always looked clumsy and awkward, back when he was a farmer, when he handled the bun tin or the punch glasses, and when he took his bicycle out. Now, those hands were ripping apart the bottom of his pants. His threadbare pants tore all the way to the knees and became raggedy, and Father's legs, thinner than his hands, were revealed. He wasn't conscious of what he was doing. It was a stubborn fight. The old, fuzzy bits of cloth piled up by the handful on the floor.

Nobody Waited

Mrs. Kim was the first of our neighbors to realize that Father was back. Mr. Kim had left this toy-like world ahead of Mother, so Mrs. Kim was now a widow. It was one of the many changes our neighborhood had seen in Father's absence. Even Mr. Kim's friends, Mr. Choe and Mr. Gwak, had stopped coming around as often.

But Mrs. Kim was so outgoing that it didn't seem like anything had changed. She was still sympathetic to her neighbors' plights and generous about her children's incessant snacking. She would also make crude jokes whenever she bumped into Mr. Gwak and Mr. Choe in the alleys. Even Mr. Gwak, the neighborhood wiseacre, would often stand awkwardly, not knowing what to say in return. The neighbors would sometimes forget that Mr. Kim had departed that snowy day last winter, and be fooled into thinking that he was still alive and being assisted by his cheerful wife.

"I was right," she said, coming over to our room, her face still sleepy. She sat down on the floor. "I thought it was about time . . . So, how are you?"

Father slowly moved his stiff body. He tilted his head to one side and an awkward smile flitted briefly across his face. Father looked pitiful, like a rusted machine.

"Fine . . ." He barely replied. His shoulders shook.

"It's good to have you back. Everyone says that it isn't somewhere you would want to go twice, but it's all right for a man to have been there once. Anyway, it's useless to think about it. You have to think about taking care of your kids. If it weren't for our children, wouldn't we all be dead by now? Come, let's go to my house. I'll make you some breakfast."

Father didn't move. He just clenched his jaws, as if he were chewing on a tough piece of arrowroot. What was it that was stuck between his teeth? I left the room ahead of them. I could hear Mrs. Kim. "Oh, stop it. If everyone in this alley were like you, Mr. Jang, there would be a big flood."

From the end of the narrow and dirty alley, the summer morning's reddish sunlight inched forward for the first time in a long while. I leisurely headed for the tofu factory. I didn't want to think about anything, even Father's return. When I told Sister the news, she looked blank for a second, but then returned to work. I couldn't breathe; the five- or six-*pyeong* workroom was filled with hot steam. Tofu Flesh's four brothers ground beans diligently, and water boiled in the large cast-iron pot. Sister, now as plump as Tofu Flesh, looked as pretty as a newlywed. Blocks of tofu with straight ends dropped from her hands and sank into the water tank.

"What's going on? Who's come back?" one of the brothers asked me, never stopping.

I didn't answer. The brother who had lost a leg in the war was there too. My future brother-in-law was silent as usual, concentrating on the task at hand. I remembered his rusted-gun smell. But I wouldn't have to smell him ever again. Sister would also never smell like that. I figured that Sister would have to come home now. That was the only thing that reassured me. "You have to come quick," I lied easily. "He said I should bring you back, with all your things."

Sister, who hadn't erased her blank expression, finally stopped and turned to face me. She quietly wiped her wet hands on her apron. For some reason, her face was red. I stuck out my tongue at her inwardly, thinking she had no choice but to come home, but I was discouraged. I suddenly remembered something.

Where is he now?
He's at the railway embankment.
Where is he now?
He's in the alley.
Where is he now?

I thought back to the many nights Sister and I had waited for Father. But our wait had always ended with disappointment. The rattling of the secondhand bicycle never reached our ears, which were open to the deepest parts of the night. Perhaps our ardent longing died along with Mother. So Father's belated return this morning seemed rather useless to Sister—maybe even to me. Nobody was waiting anymore. The people who had sincerely waited for Father were no longer in this world. Completely deflated, I turned back slowly.

Night Market

I don't think there was a new transaction between Tofu Flesh's mother and Father. We had already been paid, and Father wasn't clever enough at math to protest. Nothing changed, even though Father was finally home. Sister still lived at the tofu factory and became plumper and plumper, like Tofu Flesh, and came by our kitchen briefly once or twice a day. I didn't need to go see her to fill my stomach anymore. But because of the hallucinatory smell of the rusted gun I kept sensing, I hardly ever ate the food she made. For some reason, it had become more sickening to me since Father came home. I disliked her even more. I usually ate outside, and if I couldn't, I went to bed hungry. At those times, I was glad to be accustomed to hunger.

Before Father came back, my heart was always at home. It guarded our empty room as I ran around outside. I would rush home, even after having been immersed in Tae-gil's room, the third-rate cinema at the edge of the city, or the fun nightly hunts. I hurried home every night because I had to wait. I wasn't waiting only for Father. I waited for Sister. I was also waiting for Mother, who would never return to this world. I vaguely waited for many other things as well. From time to time, my waiting was rewarded in my dreams. For example, Father, Sister, and even Mother would be sitting in the moving truck, rattling toward the unknown city from our home in the country. In the streets where we had briefly set up shop, Father would be there with the punch jar on top of the wooden cart, Sister would be baking the red-bean buns redolent of baking soda, and Mother would be transporting buckets of metallic water. My family was together. Despite eking out a living in an unfamiliar city in a bumbling manner, we weren't discontent. Upon waking, I would expect unconsciously that we would return to our former life when Father came home.

But it was his return that ultimately shattered my expectations. It became clear that nothing, not Sister or Mother or anything else, would revert to the way it had been. Even though it was an obvious fact, I felt an immense betrayal at its confirmation. My heart didn't want to guard our empty room. I left as soon as the sun rose and returned late at night. Running around like a dog, I spent the entire day in the streets, the park, the cinema, and in the marketplace.

I met honest Gimpy around this time. I can still draw him accurately from memory. His head was abnormally large compared to his frail body, and his eyes bulged. He made rounds at various inns, wading through the damp dawn fog, a shoeshine kit over his shoulder and a portable stool at his side, limping along as if he were dancing.

The rainy season was over, but our nightly hunts went nowhere, betraying our expectations. The passion for the hunt never came back. Many more kids skipped it, and even the older boys were half-hearted about it. It might have been because of the heat, which became oppressive with the end of the rainy season. We would gather at the railroad tracks and sing dirty songs, throw rocks at the sky, and then disperse. The older boys became more cantankerous around this time as well.

I went to the night market when we didn't hunt. The market filled a wide road in front of the public stadium. If I borrowed the adults' description, the market had everything, but nothing really good. But in my eyes, it was a place filled with everything in the world. Wooden trays displayed various foods. The market sold donated used clothes and daily necessities—mostly of American origin, not Korean—and saw many drunks and whores, who multiplied as the night deepened. I felt hungry around that time, since I had been running around the city all day. I wanted all the food on the wooden trays. Whale meat and sardines broiling on the grill, mung-bean pancakes and Chinese buns sizzling in greased pans, dough-flake soup, tiny rice balls, and mung-bean porridge in jars—I went around looking at all of these, with their different shapes, colors, and smells, water gathering in my mouth. It seemed that others were interested in food as well. The food merchants had the most customers. I envied the customers' enormous appetites. From the poor A-frame carrier to the women holding shopping baskets, they packed around the wooden trays and devoured everything in sight. Whenever I stood there looking at them, it seemed as if the residents of the city were living each day to briefly satisfy their tongues. My small stomach seemed to fill up just by watching them.

The Chinese bun shop near the entrance of the market always burst at the seams with customers. For some reason, everyone, even if he were the mayor, had to stand in line for those buns. Even when another Chinese bun shop nearby had no customers, this one was always mobbed, for very good reasons. First of all, it was the size of the buns. For the majority of residents, who hadn't filled their stomachs to their liking in a long while, this was a selling point that couldn't be overlooked. It was a time when people chose quantity over quality. Even if they had been made of dirt, those Chinese buns would have been a satisfactory size. "How can they go on, even with quick sales at small profits?" Some customers would worry about the owner's business acumen. "They're going to have to sell land to keep making Chinese buns . . ." According to rumors, however, the owner bought land by selling buns.

Of course, the biggest reason why everyone loved those buns was because they tasted good. They really could have melted my tongue. They had the same ingredients as every other bun—flour, yeast, baking soda, saccharin, and a red bean and sweet potato filling—but there must have been a secret addictive ingredient. Even I, who had made red-bean buns once, couldn't figure out what it was. So a rumor went around, alleging that they put something secret in their batter. According to someone who claimed he had checked it out, it was snake powder. "You would know how good it is if you've tried snake powder. Even a barley cake tastes great if you just sprinkle some on . . ."

That shop had three grills, made of oil drums cut in half. The bald, doughy owner in his fifties and two women, most probably his wife and daughter, would bake them ceaselessly, sweat falling freely from their faces, but customers still lined up outside. They were able to relax only when they were about to close the shop late into the night, and they would give the leftovers to kids with dirty hands, clothes, and sometimes even hearts, who hadn't been able to tear themselves away. Then all the urchins would stick out their small, filthy hands, and shout, me too, me too! Thinking of last winter, I would blush. At no other time did my history of begging make me feel so ashamed. Of course I wanted to stick my hand out too. But I was infuriated with the behavior of those shameless kids and wanted to kick them. Sometimes I even felt like burning up that kind-hearted owner's bun shop.

Tae-gil was a good friend. He would steal instead of sticking his hand out, and he would rather wrest it away from a weaker kid than steal. He was proud. So I never came back empty-handed whenever I went with him. Korean melons, at their peak around that time, raw corn or summer potato, *senbei* cookies sprinkled with strips of fragrant seaweed, a handful of aromatic, fluffy Vietnamese rice—we could fill our stomachs by going around the market once. Of course, I never kicked the kids or set fire to the Chinese bun shop. I would bow my head, push down the curses boiling up inside me, and turn around powerlessly. Once, someone stopped me. It was the shoe-shine boy Gimpy.

"You live in the shantytown, right?" he asked. I blushed, feeling as if I couldn't take it anymore. I glared at him.

"I live there too," he said, shifting his shoeshine kit.

I thought he looked familiar. *But so what?* I replied roughly, "So what?"

"Nothing." He smiled feebly, and that pushed me over the edge. I decided that he had thought I was one of the begging kids, and was laughing because I hadn't gotten any buns. I threw myself on him. Our fight didn't last long. Even though he was crippled, he was two years older than I and didn't want to fight. Plus, since we were at the market, a showdown befitting my feelings would have been impossible. Our fight ended lamely, with both of us getting rapped on the head by a few adults.

"Hey, do you want to shine shoes with me?" Gimpy asked on the way home, limping next to me.

The Bag You Can
Travel the World with

The next afternoon, Gimpy made my shoeshine kit and stool from two apple crates without any tools to speak of. Even though he was a shoeshine boy, perhaps he would grow up to be a well-respected carpenter like drunkard Ju, although his crippled leg could be a problem. To be honest, after he spent an afternoon making them, I found it unbearable to take them and go out into the streets. It seemed impossible. "It's no big deal. Just follow me," Gimpy encouraged me, sanding the outside of the new shoeshine kit and making it look worn with shoe polish. "Hey, with this, nobody will think that you're new. It's pretty good. We're two boy-shiners starting tomorrow." He grinned. It was the same smile that had angered me the day before. Instead of anger, I felt friendship.

The next morning, when he came to pick me up, I still hadn't made a decision. But since it was too late to get out of it, I went along. The shoeshine kit over my shoulder and the stool under my arm dragged me down. I'd felt less self-conscious when I walked around with the mess kit. As soon as we left the shantytown, Gimpy left me and crossed over to the other side of the road. He started shouting, "Shine your shoes!" and lumbered downtown. *Yeah, we're two boy-shiners*, I thought to myself, embarrassed. I would have to do the same if I wanted to fulfill my duties as a business partner. Gimpy shouted enthusiastically, "Shine your shoes! Shine your shoooes!" But it wasn't easy for me. My heart felt as if it would burst from the pressure, and my throat closed up. Everyone on the streets, even inanimate objects, seemed to be scrutinizing me. It would have been more natural to walk around with my dick exposed like Tae-gil than with this burdensome shoeshine kit. I felt bad for my business partner, but I could only follow him silently.

We found our first customer. Despite Gimpy's energy and experience, I had struck a deal first. Frightened, I hurriedly beckoned my business partner over. Of course, I had been briefed adequately beforehand. Still, when the middle-aged man sat down on the stool and put one foot on each of our kits, I panicked. If I had followed my teacher's instructions, I should have first brushed off the dirt on the bottom of his sole with a toothbrush, dusted his shoe, cleaned it, put polish on it, and shined it. But I was so nervous that I slathered the polish on before brushing off the dirt, and, more panicked because of my mistake, I even missed and dabbed shoe polish on the customer's clean sock.

"Kid, you must be new," the customer said, looking down at me as I fumbled. I didn't reply. My face burned.

Gimpy, stealing a careful look at the customer to gauge his mood, quickly said, "It's only been three days since he started. I'll clean that shoe after I finish with this one, so please don't worry."

I didn't have the courage to lift my head. But the gentleman didn't seem annoyed at my mistake. "Of course," he said. "Shining shoes is a great skill, and not easy to master from the beginning. Do you know what I did as soon as I decided to come down south? I went around with cobblers and learned how to repair shoes. You have to have at least one kind of skill to survive wherever you find yourself. I thought that repairing shoes is a skill I could use no matter where I found myself. It's not difficult, and you don't need much to start up. If you had a tool kit, you can at least make enough to survive. It's the same with shining shoes. If you have a shoeshine kit, you can travel all over the world, so it's a great skill . . ." He told us more about life. Now that I think of it, we were hearing the most valuable economics lecture: about survival, money, jobs, and people.

I finally mustered the courage to look up at his face. He was smiling gently at me. My heart felt as if it would burst. I concentrated on the shoe again. I diligently brushed it, rubbed polish on it, and shined it with spit. Sweat dropped onto the tip of his shoe. But I couldn't catch up to Gimpy's experience in one day. Despite all of my efforts, the shoe I shined couldn't be compared to my partner's. But the gentleman didn't care. He refused Gimpy's offer to redo it. "You don't have to do that. It's something you stick your smelly feet into, not a medal. It's fine. Good job, both of you." Wearing his mismatched shoes, he left in a hurry.

Rough Sex

We left home at dawn. Gimpy knocked on our door as soon as the curfew ended, saying that we had to go and make money. Father never said anything. He would only look sleepily out at his son industriously leaving the dark alley, and yawn lazily. We were about to make rounds at inns. Gimpy kept urging me to hurry, saying that we had to beat the other kids to it. If we started late, he made us run. Our two shoeshine kits would rattle loudly. "Those other kids are hard workers. These days they're always getting there early. Hurry up!" he would say, huffing. His crippled leg seemed stronger than my own normal one. Running after him, I would often think of random things.

Once, I remembered the way we used to go around gathering persimmon flowers. In the country, we kids wouldn't be able to sleep around the time persimmon flowers bloomed. Sometimes we would leave our homes in the middle of the night, rubbing our eyes sleepily. Sister and I would go on a pilgrimage to all the paths in our village, checking every persimmon tree. Small persimmon flowers would be carpeting the ground under unvisited trees. We would also wake up in the middle of the night during the time of year when the sound of ripe persimmons falling and rolling on the ground could be heard. We would rush out as soon as the rooster crowed and gather enough persimmons to fill a big basket or a rough straw sack.

We couldn't hit every single inn in the city, no matter how diligent we were. The places we could go to were limited. We were able to frequent the seedy inns near the market or the train station. People were in every room in those kinds of establishments, and shoes, whether they were men's or women's, were flung carelessly in front of each door. Gimpy was as precise and quick as a machine. Even shoes in the worst shape could be spruced up in five minutes. But I needed at least twenty minutes. We had so little time in which to work that I could almost see the time pass. As we ran around crazily, the morning sun, dyeing one side of the city's sky orange, would warm our foreheads.

We were supposed to split our income in half since we were business partners. I obviously felt indebted to Gimpy. Clearly, the workload had to be as fair as the distribution of earnings. After much thought, I suggested that I would bring the shoes to him while he did the cleaning. This was also judged to be more efficient, so we soon tried it. But I was slow even at this. Gimpy's speed in cleaning the shoes was almost always constant. Unfortunately, so many unexpected events awaited me. Nobody staying at an inn went to bed early. If I woke someone up, I wouldn't be able to get any shoes. The mean proprietor would slap me if I bumped into him. Sometimes I would be accused of being a thief, and then I would be strip-searched. Tact and courage were necessary for this work, but even so, there were times when I couldn't get anything.

When I returned with nothing, my business partner would hit the side of his kit and yell, "None? Just bring them all here. Don't ask them! I'm sure they don't only have rubber shoes!" I never resented that honest Gimpy. All he did was to encourage his timid partner, and I could only blame my lack of skills and the day's luck. Blushing, I would have to run into another establishment.

Actually, the hardest part for me lay elsewhere. Even when the city was in deep sleep, some women wandered in the alleys. Some would be inside a room into which you could see as if it were a display case, dejectedly checking their fortunes. At times a useless drunk and a hardscrabble woman would fight in the middle of the night, and all kinds of rough phrases would be thrown about. All inns were like that, but it was especially the case for the ones near the market or the train station. It was even worse in the red-light district. I had even seen a woman wearing nothing but panties walking out barefoot as if she were sleepwalking, peeing in the narrow cement yard, then crawling back into her hole to sleep. I witnessed all kinds of raunchy behavior other than that, but there's no reason to go into detail. My young heart was often overwhelmed by the hardship of living, the roughness, and the impudence. But I still remember what Gimpy said once: "It's normal for them. They're the kind of people who have no shame . . ."

I had to return to the places where I hadn't found business earlier. It might have been because of the heat; all the people seemed to have given up covering even their private parts. There wasn't any reason for me to hide since I was only rooting around for other people's shoes. I fearlessly waded through the naked people, looking for work. Nobody intervened. Those places were generous to kids like us.

I bumped into Tough Widow's daughter in one of those inns. She was sitting next to a sleeping man, calmly smoking. The small door was open in the intense heat, and I could see the cave-like interior in one glance. I thought of Tough Widow's son-in-law. The good-looking guy, who lived off her but picked fights with her in the middle of the night, was the laughingstock of the neighborhood, but frequented Gang's Barbershop the most. I checked the sleeping man's face. It wasn't him. "Clean those shoes," she said. I said I would. She had only the smallest pieces of fabric draping her body, so I could see all of her—her pale face, thin neck, and frail body. Her health was worse than I had thought. She was always late coming home from a bar. Whenever I saw her weaving through the alleys with the curfew siren behind her, I was edgy because her tired and drunken gait looked so frail. And I knew that the only things waiting for her were a box-like room, her mother, known to be tougher than ten men, and the good-for-nothing man who did nothing except to complain every night that she wasn't sleeping with him. Two pairs of shoes were lying around in front of the door. One pair was hers, the other the man's. When I picked up both pairs, she said, "No, just that one." I took only her shoes, small and worn-out like herself, and turned back. I realized that I felt fine, even though I had bumped into her in a place like this. I wasn't surprised or shocked. Feeling calm, I tossed them in front of Gimpy.

After our rounds, we ate a late breakfast at our favorite eatery. This was where we each ordered double portions of *kake udon* and split our earnings equally. I was ambivalent every time. One was the feeling of wanting more, even after having eaten a double portion of *kake udon*, unable to forget its taste. The other was my guilty conscience for splitting the money equally. But I never could resolve this conflict before leaving the eatery. That day I had an additional conflict, about Tough Widow's daughter. I felt as if I were her accomplice even though she hadn't recognized me.

Turf

My shoeshine kit was just that, not a way to travel the world. It wasn't long before I realized it. The last summer heat wave raged on. The asphalt roads downtown melted like taffy and there were fewer people out in the middle of the day. The city seemed to be locked in a cannon-roarless war with the murderous heat. It was obvious which side would win. The stores had drawn their window shades, covered the display case windows with newspaper, and hosed down the sidewalk, but that wasn't enough to block out the steaming heat. Everything exposed to the sun burned red, like a whole chicken tossed into boiling oil. Naturally, people seemed to have become rougher and drier.

I was alone. Once our work at dawn was done, our partnership dissolved. From this point we acted alone. This was, of course, Gimpy's suggestion. It was so that he could earn a little more, and I wasn't in a position to object to that. We always parted ways in front of our eatery, and I would feel useless and lonely from then on. Unlike Gimpy, I wasn't intent on earning more money. I didn't think anything would change even if I earned more than my partner. I had needed more money a long time ago, before Sister went to

Tofu Flesh's house, before Mother died, and before Father became an ex-convict.

Father had started earning money a little while ago. He had needed less capital to start than I had. He only needed an A-frame haphazardly hammered together from wooden sticks. So we didn't need my money. After a lot of thought, I made a small box with a hole on the top and put my daily earnings in it. But I didn't have a purpose for the money, so after dropping it in the box I would forget that it was there.

I would spend the rest of the day killing time. I wandered around the streets with my shoeshine kit over my shoulder. I could now shout, "Shine your shoes!" "Shine your shoooes!" but walked around with my mouth shut.

I didn't really know how the war had swept through this city. The things I had seen thus far had been remaining scars. A wrecked transport warehouse, a half-burned community building, a few bare steel towers used for who-knows-what, the dirty creek that was said to have been used as a burial ground for many soldiers and civilians, the bald park where unemployed refugees milled about. People got murdered in broad daylight in the Yankee market in front of the train station. All kinds of lowly regional dialects made a din in the rough-and-tumble pebble-filled yard. Skirting around those places, I was a scared spectator.

My bare feet inside my rubber shoes were very hot and slippery with sweat. I found a patch of shade and sat on my kit. I felt dizzy. A starving dog, his long red tongue hanging out, inched along the empty street, panting. I closed my eyes. My eyelids burned up in red, and the city moaned *wooah wooah* as if it would explode like an overheated blast furnace. I must have dozed off. When I opened my eyes, two army boots were planted firmly in front of me. I looked up. Perched on the stool, a young man in a shirt was looking at me. I quickly pulled the kit from under myself. That was a mistake. He kicked the kit, and the various objects inside were strewn all around.

"Go pick them up!"

I did. He ordered, "Sit down! And give me your hand."

I showed him my right hand.

"Seems like you did pretty well. My kids are just sitting around, yawning." He flipped my smudged hand over a few times. The next moment, I screamed, not having realized his plan. My hand was smashed under his thick shoe.

"Shut up, before I crush it," he said coldly, his foot still on my hand. "Tell me, why are you working here? Who gave you permission? You think this is your front yard? This is my turf. Get it, you little fucker?"

I couldn't say anything. It was entirely my fault. I had forgotten Gimpy's instructions for an instant. When we parted in front of our eatery, he would always emphasize: first, I should never veer away from our usual route, and second, if I had to go through someone else's territory, I should take a detour along the edges.

Of all the city's streets, there were very few places kids like us could go. You could get into a lot of trouble if you didn't adhere to the boundaries. Also, even in the allowed areas, there were still parts that were off-limits: the famous tearooms or public buildings, the always-busy plaza in front of the train station, or near the cross-country bus terminal, where the turf kings reigned, collecting expensive rents. Of course, I didn't know who the turf kings were.

I knew they weren't the tearoom owners, the heads of the public organizations, or the presidents of the bus companies. It was clear, however, that the man I had encountered was one.

I didn't resist, but I also didn't beg for forgiveness. His foot still crushing my hand, he asked, "So what are you going to do? Want me to break your hand so that you will never work again?"

Realizing what he wanted, I obediently gave him what I'd earned that day. He quickly took it and my hand was finally freed from its shackles. My five fingers were squashed and bruised.

"Hey, kid," he addressed me gently, getting up and patting my shoulder genially, "Don't ever show your face around here. Please, kid, it's hard for both of us." With real pain in his face he crossed the road and walked away in the scorching sun. I stood up with the bag with which I couldn't ever travel the world. My hand hurt, but I didn't feel bad.

That night, we hunted. The prey caught in our trap wasn't as big an opponent as Big Nose, but he was close. The hunt was successful as usual, and we were satisfied.

Under Renovation

T ae-gil was the first to tell me about the events that unfolded at Gang's Barbershop. It happened during the day, when I was wandering around the city with my shoeshine kit.

Our earnings were pretty good that day. We didn't encounter any problems during the early morning hours and there was quite a constant flow throughout the day. It made me feel good, even though I didn't care much about making money. I turned into our alley when darkness was starting to settle in lightly. The oppressive smell of burning coal powder, coal, and sawdust spread over the alley. With the heat wave over, the summer evening was pleasant. I saw familiar people going home, their gait revealing their fatigue.

Tae-gil had been waiting for me impatiently. He rushed over from the other side and bumped into me as I headed toward our room. He was extremely excited.

"You're finally here! I just went to your house," he panted, unable to find the right words.

"Why?"

"It happened again! At Gang's Barbershop!" he cried, out of breath.

"Oh, that's it? You scared me for nothing," I replied, nonchalantly. I thought he meant that a new opponent had appeared. But that wasn't news. It was as old as our nightly hunts. I was indifferent despite his excitement. Similar to our always-defeated victims, we had never seen anyone who had won against Mr. Kang. I thought the result was obvious, so I asked, still uninterested, "So who's the guy who got beaten this time?"

"Not just beaten," he said, shivering. He said in a strange low voice, "He's dead. It's true. I saw him, and there's no way he's going to live. He's really dead."

"What? Who?" I asked, suddenly serious. "Who died? Not Mr. Kang, right?"

"Don't be shocked. Mr. Kang, the owner of Gang's Barbershop, is dead."

"Mr. Kang? Are you sure? Did you really see him? Are you joking?"

I finally sobered and asked the same thing a few more times. But Tae-gil wasn't joking. Trembling with excitement, he wanted to go to the shop right away. I couldn't believe it. Had the mysterious Mr. Kang, our idol, finally fallen? We ran toward Gang's Barbershop. The barbershop was locked and dark. There wasn't a single spectator. The barbershop was empty, as if it had been closed early. Only the fixtures were inside, sunk in darkness. I felt a horrifying chill trickling down my spine. It was as if the summer night's gentleness had wrapped around my neck to strangle me like a wet towel. I noticed a couple of strange things. The appliances inside weren't orderly as they usually were. Like the way kids push all the desks and chairs to the back wall to clean the classroom, everything was piled up in a corner. But it didn't seem like there had been a cleaning. A few clumps of hair that hadn't yet been swept away were scattered on the empty cement floor, as well as a few broken wooden bars. That was it; none of the appliances seemed to have been damaged. Nothing, except for the early closing and a note stuck near the doorknob, appeared different from the outside. I read the words on the hand-sized note: "Under renovation, business closed until further notice." I turned around, dumbfounded. My entire body broke out in goose bumps.

Tae-gil told me that a group of five or six men, wearing unseasonable jackets in the heat, came into Gang's Barbershop right after lunchtime. They locked the door behind them as soon as they stepped inside. As was usually the case at that time of day, there weren't any customers. Mr. Kang was, as usual, sitting on a chair turned toward the window, gazing outside leisurely. Perhaps he had even dozed off. The other two barbers and the female beautician were flipping through the newspaper and listening to a drama on the radio. The intruders disturbed their peace. The men each took out a wooden bar from their jackets. According to one employee, the rough bars smelled strongly of resin, as if they had just been cut off at the sawmill. Strangely, Mr. Kang was helpless. Although the men had a head start, nobody would have expected that to happen. One man turned up the volume of the radio. The drama, a true story about the war, was recreating a fierce fight scene. All kinds of gunfire, the deafening noise of a tank, and the screams of people in their death throes filled the shop, and a merciless terror was committed against this backdrop.

I heard that while Mr. Kang looked bluish, like a dead man, a cold smile played on his lips. The men pushed everything into a corner and pulled Mr. Kang off his chair. He didn't resist. He was quiet, as if he knew his place. A few men stood in front of the windows to block them and the employees were forced to stand facing the wall. The fighting heated up on the radio. Amid the gunfire and tank and bomber noises, the employees clearly heard the most primitive violence being cruelly inflicted on Mr. Kang. When the men left, only a few broken wooden bars and Mr. Kang's ruined body were crumpled on the floor. He was moved to the hospital, but nobody expected him to survive. It seemed impossible that he would mysteriously ward off the invaders and reclaim his kingdom, as he had done before.

A week later, the barbershop reopened its doors. Despite the note about the renovation, nothing had changed. The only changes were that the female beautician wasn't there anymore and that the sign was new. Instead of Kang's Barbershop, the new sign said Hope Barbershop. Two new employees soon replaced the female beautician. We would often see the new owner, a dark-complexioned man in a jacket and pointy-toed shoes. Located on a busy alley, the barbershop was fairly successful. Every time I passed by, I would look at the sign that said Hope Barbershop. Instead of hope, I felt a dark, empty despair. I thought often of Mr. Gwak's words about the queen ant and the soldier ant. According to his explanations, it would only mean that the queen ant had traded one soldier ant for another. But I couldn't comprehend the cruel and strange order of that world.

Tofu Flesh and the Older Boys

I wasn't the only one who was shocked by Mr. Kang's death. I'm certain that we were all enormously conflicted by his death. Nobody realized its true magnitude, though, because our turmoil was too large and deep for our comprehension.

I became even less enthusiastic about my work. If the diligent Gimpy hadn't come to wake me every morning, I would have thrown away the useless shoeshine kit—with which you could never travel the world—a long time ago.

We were bored with our hunts as well. One by one, we gathered at the railroad tracks each night, out of habit and because of our thirst, but we weren't as excited as we had been before. We didn't hunt very often. Even if we did, we got involved only half-heartedly. Nobody volunteered to be bait anymore, and we would release the victims without harassing them. We had no use for the fun of the hunt, which had completely captivated us before. Sitting in a row on the railroad tracks in the dark, we would grumble that everything was dull. The older boys were the same. Perhaps they were to blame for the lifeless atmosphere. You couldn't find from them the passion of conducting roll call at each gathering or the earnestness with which they had orchestrated plans. The passion that had enveloped them for so long was gone, mutated into something boring and lame. We younger kids were picked on often because of their mysterious depression and irritation. They would strip Tae-gil, the way his mother would, if he didn't bring them cigarettes, or kick one of us hard if we complained.

We became more and more frightened of the older boys, whom we had trusted and followed more than we did our own parents at one point. We tried to stay as far away from them as possible. I can't explain why we gathered at the railroad tracks in spite of all that. Even though this might be taken the wrong way—and anyway it's a vague way to describe it—all I can say is that it was probably because of our thirst. We craved something that would gently embrace our poor, starving, and abused souls—love. It was the deep thirst that came with the lack of love.

The older boys started talking about Sister around then. It was because of Tofu Flesh. Sitting on the tracks, they were sipping liquor out of the bottle. It was after most of the kids had gone home, since it was very late and we hadn't gone on a hunt. A few kids, including myself, were still there studying them, having nothing else to do. Summer seemed to be already over. The night was a little chilly. The older boys' cigarettes flashed brightly in the night. They felt warm at this time of year. But the light went out quickly, and we were left only with the older boys' laughter and the empty darkness. One of them took his thing out and played with it. Because of his act and the boys' drunkenness, their depression quickly turned naughty.

"Oh my god!"

We looked up and saw someone running away into the darkness. It was a girl.

"Get her!" shouted the boy who had been playing with himself, and the other older boys gave chase. We followed them in the confusion of the moment. She was caught only a few feet away. It was Tofu Flesh. I recognized her even in the darkness.

"You want to get killed? Why are you snooping around?" The boy who had been playing with himself shoved a broken bottle in her face, as if he would swipe it at her any moment. He trembled with humiliation.

But Tofu Flesh was nonchalant. She befriended more boys than girls probably on account of her white plumpness, and she wasn't intimidated. She replied confidently, "I wasn't! Why are you doing that kind of dirty thing anyway?"

"What? I'm going to kill you!"

We held our breaths. I imagined her falling to the ground screaming, holding her blood-covered face. But the boy hesitated. He trembled, at a crossroads sharper than the broken bottle. It was quite an urgent situation. We were tense, thinking that we had to intervene for him, who was stuck between humiliation and immense destruction.

She broke the balance. "Stop being stupid and get this away from me!" she said in a cold, low voice. It was the most scorn-filled voice a woman could utter to a man. "Act like a man, you coward."

The bottle shattered into pieces. At the same time, the two fell into the weeds next to the tracks. She screamed a couple of times but soon became quiet. Darkness and silence covered everything. The older boys, who had been as still as statues, suddenly shooed us away, laughing. Chased far away without knowing why, we threw a few stones toward them. We couldn't hear their laughter anymore.

A-frame

Like me, who had no interest in earning money, Father didn't
seem determined to make a living. He left home daily with
the A-frame on his back and I left home with the kit over my shoulder. I left at dawn because of the industrious Gimpy, but Father was
a bit lazier. Also, he would return home earlier than I did, so the
first thing I saw upon returning home was the empty A-frame. It
wasn't even made from the usual A-frame wood, but rather haphazardly from a few pieces of wooden bars bought at the sawmill. It
should have been called a city A-frame, since it was as slipshod as its
owner. I had seen Father returning with it on his back a few times.
Head bent, he would walk down the long, narrow alley with only
one shoulder strap secured on his shoulder. Everything about the
picture screamed carelessness. His gait, bent head, the swaying A-
frame hanging to one side, his limp fingers just barely holding onto
his dragging walking stick, the toy-like shacks, and the long and
narrow alley—everything looked slovenly, haphazard, and foolish.
Everything was made carelessly, and just imagining Father wandering the streets, or around the marketplace and train station like that
made me want to laugh.

It was only natural that Father wasn't enthusiastic about making money. Father hadn't been good with the A-frame even when we were living in the country. If he shouldered a stack of wood, his pile would be only half as tall as the others', and it would also be tilted to one side, making people laugh. He went out every day to make a living in this cold-hearted city with his clumsy skills. I think the result would have been the same even if he concentrated on making money. Even if we hadn't taken his clumsiness into consideration, I had never heard of anyone—at least in our shantytown—who became rich by working a lame A-frame. Plenty of neighbors earned their living from the same thing, and I often saw them walking drunkenly back home, a few old scabbard fish hanging from their A-frames. I knew that those were lucky days. It may have been fortunate that someone like Father never expected much from his A-frame.

I hadn't forgotten Father's failure at selling red-bean buns when we first got to the city. Not knowing much back then, Father had said confidently, greasing the twenty-four-holed bun tin with clumsy hands, "Just wait and see. This contraption will start printing a lot of bills." Since then, Father had learned how hard it was to angle for other people's money in this harsh world. So you couldn't criticize him for not caring about the A-frame, which wasn't any better an instrument than the bun tin. But he earned less because he was lazy, and he became lazier because he didn't make much.

Father went over to Mr. Kim's room almost every night. Even though its owner was dead, his friends had started coming by again. The voices of Mr. Gwak, Mr. Choe, Mrs. Kim, and now Father would blend together, and their laughter wouldn't stop until late into the night. Sometimes their group disbanded way after midnight, and on those nights Father, who would come home with hollow eyes, would sit, leaning against the wall, and heave deep sighs. It wasn't that I didn't understand Father's despair. I just didn't ever want to join in, so I would face the other way, curled up like a shrimp, and pretend I was asleep. Father would keep sighing in bed, would even moan a bit, before finally falling asleep.

A chunk of the tedious afternoons had gone with the heat. One day, when the day seemed shorter than ever, I turned into our alley and realized that Father's A-frame wasn't there. Our room was dark and not a sound came out from the Kims' across the alley. I thought it was strange. Perhaps Father had gone out with the A-frame again, to extricate himself of the despair that didn't let him sleep at night. I waited for him in our room, which was also unusual. I recalled the nights Sister and I had waited up for him. I felt hollow. A vague but urgent feeling seized me for a while. Father returned quite late, but I didn't ask why. The reason was obvious. Father quickly brought in the bundles he had lugged with difficulty, and it was, surprisingly, multicolored bolts of fabric. His face, shining with sweat, had a strange expression I had never seen before. I didn't dare look at him.

"Don't tell anyone," he told me, his voice thick. He went over to the Kims'. Soon, he brought back Mrs. Kim and Mr. Gwak. They all took a couple of bolts out from the heap of fabric and left. Father didn't come home even after midnight. Mrs. Kim's room was quiet. I could only hear the tired snores of our neighbors. I tried to go to sleep, curled up tightly, but I couldn't. At that moment, Sister came in. She looked surprised at Father's absence and the presence of unfamiliar goods. But she was clearly feeling something stronger and more wrenching. Or maybe she understood everything in a glance.

As she did every time she came over in the middle of the night, she lay down without saying a word. She turned away from me, curled up, and started to weep silently. It was a very deep and tenacious crying, the kind that burned away the sorrow from the inside. But the unpleasant rusted-gun smell was still there. Sister cried for a long time, but this time her tears couldn't wash away the smell.

I finally fell asleep near dawn, but only for a little while. I soon woke up with everyone else because of the commotion coming from Tough Widow's room.

"Why aren't you giving it to me? What kind of man would leave a bitch alone if she doesn't give her pussy?"

"You want to act like a man, even though you're living off a woman? If that's such a problem, why don't you find a hole in the wall to bang? You useless piece of shit!"

Mother-in-law and son-in-law fought, while the thin, pale woman, whom I'd bumped into in an inn at dawn once, cried pathetically.

Judas's Hour

W hen Gimpy came to get me, I finally thought of something I had to do: smashing my shoeshine kit. It had been useless to me from the beginning. I had lugged it around every day for no reason. Gimpy was standing alone in the damp dawn. The morning fog felt cold to the skin. "Hey, we're late. Hurry up," he said, his voice sleepy. "Sorry, I overslept. Come on."

A while ago, he had started going to the Sunday school, where they taught upper-grade elementary school lessons and conducted Bible study for a few hours every evening. He attended diligently. It was too much for him, especially with his disability, so he grew more and more tired. He came later and later to wake me, which he used to do as soon as the curfew was over, and he would often stifle yawns on the job.

Gimpy looked more tired than ever, and his crippled leg seemed weaker as well. I couldn't bring myself to tell him my decision, as he was my business partner and a kind teacher. I told him I didn't feel well, but because he looked so worried, I changed my story and said that there was something I had to do. I promised him that I would fill him in on the details later in the evening. His face clouded over, he finally turned away, feet dragging. He slowly limped out the alley covered by damp fog. I turned around, as downcast as Gimpy. I felt guilty, and decided that I would keep my false promise to him.

Morning sunlight shone in through the hand-sized window, brightening our small box-like room. Tofu Flesh came to get Sister, who had been immobile. Sister left the room without saying anything. Her unknown sorrow, which had driven her out in the middle of the night and caused that persistent, ragged crying, had disappeared completely. I listened to their whispers and giggles from inside the room. They left.

I did what I needed to when I was alone. It was easy and liberating. I placed the shoeshine kit on the kitchen floor and smashed it to bits with a hammer. I didn't leave anything inside intact. After I swept the crushed pieces into the garbage can, Father's slipshod A-frame came into view. I wanted to smash that too, but didn't. After all, it was Father's.

Father was busy all day. He, along with Mrs. Kim and Mr. Gwak, kept going in and out of our room. Not a single bolt of fabric was left by the end of the day. I left home when darkness filled our alley. Loud laughter, belonging to Mrs. Kim, Mr. Gwak, Mr. Choe, and Father, came from Mrs. Kim's room. Among them, Father's laughter was the loudest and the emptiest. I remembered something from when we had lived in the country. Passers-by would recognize Father's laughter, no matter whose house he was laughing in. But now that laughter didn't reverberate with me.

Sister was hard at work. Tofu Flesh's four brothers were there too, grinding beans in the steamy workroom. Sister was drenched in sweat, but her expression was brighter than ever before. *She's happy again.* With that one-legged man who smelled of rusted gun.

The last thing I did in the toy-like shantytown in that ridiculous city was to visit Gimpy at the tent school on top of the hill. Darkness and wind surrounded the pioneer church, with its two old army tents and a makeshift belfry. I went toward the tent that had a sign saying, "Grace of God Bible Club." Some ten kids were sitting on the wooden floor. They were mostly kids I knew from my shantytown. I could see Gimpy and the profile of the girl who had had a seizure. Gimpy was dozing and the girl was in deep thought, her thin face tilted to one side.

The teacher was Reverend Cha, the one who had reassured Mother that, if she prayed to God as she did to Wise Old Goddess of Maternity, our family would be able to live together again. But Mother's wish never came true. "God never lies. The hour for our salvation hasn't come yet . . ." Reverend Cha opened the Bible and started reading. "Now when the even was come, he sat down with the twelve. And as they did eat, he said, Verily I say unto you, that one of you shall betray me—this is recorded in the Book of Matthew, 26: 20 to 21. Then Jesus said unto the chief priests, and captains of the temple, and the elders, which were come to him, Be ye out, as against a thief, with swords and staves? When I was daily with you in the temple, ye stretched forth no hands against me: but this is your hour, and the power of darkness—Amen, this is recorded in the Book of Luke, 22:52 to 53. But this is your hour, and the power of darkness. . . ."

I turned back, breaking my promise with Gimpy. Layers of darkness enveloped me. I left the school with my hands shoved deep in

my pockets and my head down. I suddenly thought of the countryside
school I used to attend. I tried hard to remember the scribbles I had
left on the sixth desk in the second row from the south windows.

Afterword

Not many novelists have written autobiographies, although many painters have left behind self-portraits. Most writers do not feel the need to pen autobiographies. They can write about themselves as if they were describing other people. I think this explains why I have devoted myself to writing fiction for the past 20 years, putting other affairs of my life on the back burner.

Toy City was written as three parts of a novella. Part One, in the same title, was published in July 1979, Part Two, "Starving Soul," in April 1980, and Part Three, "Judas's Hour," in March 1982, all in different periodicals. In other words, I struggled with the work for over three years. Whenever I write a story, I almost always find myself plunged deep in despair, dragged down by anxiety and helplessness, feeling as if I would never be able to finish it. In the throes of this unavoidable pain, I realize afresh what a ruthless form fiction is.

As I write this afterword, I hope I have managed to depict in my novella the poverty-stricken 1950s that most Koreans were forced to go through. I also wish to have painted a portrait of a woman who left us during that dark period. That era and that death awakened me to the inherent emptiness of human life. I have a feeling that I find it impossible to abandon fiction writing despite the inevitable fall into a pit of despair, mainly because it is an activity to overcome them.

Lee Dong-ha
Mokpo, South Korea, April 1982

About the Author

Dong-ha Lee was born in Gyeongsan, North Gyeongsang Province, in 1942. He studied creative writing at Sorabol Art College and received a Master's degree in Korean Literature at Konkuk University. He is currently a professor of creative writing at Chung-Ang University. Lee's works include *War and Squirrel* (Jeonjaenggwa daramjwi), 1966; *Enduring Winter*, 1967; *Sand* (Morae), 1978; *A Depressing Homecoming* (Uulhan gwihyang), 1978; *Toy City* (Jangnangam Dosi), 1982; *City Swamp* (Dosiui neup), 1979; *The House of Wind* (Barameui jip), 1979; *Study of Violence* (Pongnyeok yeongu), 1987; *In Front of the Door* (Munapeseo), 1993. He is the recipient of the Korean Fiction Award (Hanguk soseol munhak sang), 1977; Korean Literary Writer Award (Hanguk munhak jakga sang), 1983; Modern Literature Award (Hyeondai munhak sang), 1986; and O Yeong-su Literature Award, 1993.

About the Translator

Chi-Young Kim is the recipient of The Daesan Foundation Translation Grant (2005) and the 34th Modern Korean Literature Translation Award (2003). Her translations include Kim Young-ha's "Moving" (*Koreana Magazine*, 2004), Jung Mi Kyung's "Memories of Lily-Colored Photographs" (*Words Without Borders*, 2004), and Kim Young-ha's *I Have the Right to Destroy Myself* (Harvest Books, 2007).